The Save

CAMPUS CONFESSIONS
BOOK TWO

CYNTHIA GUNDERSON

With Gratitude

Editing and Critique
Jordan Truex, Scott Gunderson, Sue Prince

Cover Design
Ink and Veil

Author Note

Before I started writing *The Save*, I wanted to find a way to show how Maddie could impact the Outlaws and their season using her smarts. I started writing a story where her analytical mind was her super power. In the 1990's, data and analytics were still fringe when it came to building teams and winning championships, but it did exist. I love the idea that a student like Maddie could've figured this out on her own and started a revolution.

As I researched, I discovered that there is a woman in the real world who made waves with analytics. Meghan Chayka. She's the co-founder of Stathletes, a hockey analytics company used by NHL teams and international organizations. Stathletes tracks thousands of data points per game, providing in-depth player and team analysis far beyond traditional stats. Chayka and her team have helped bring advanced metrics into locker rooms and front offices, paving the way for a more data-driven, inclusive future in the sport.

That's the Maddie girl spirit. A brilliant mind whose insights change the game.

In crafting Maddie's character, I found myself inspired by so many real women making waves in professional hockey.

Women like:

- **Hayley Wickenheiser** – Four-time Olympic gold medalist, now Assistant General Manager of Player Development for the Toronto Maple Leafs.

- **Manon Rhéaume** – The first woman to play in an NHL game, breaking barriers as a goaltender for the Tampa Bay Lightning in a 1992 preseason match.

- **Cammi Granato** – Olympic icon and the first female pro scout for the NHL's Seattle Kraken.

- **Jessica Campbell** – Former Team Canada player turned coach, now working in professional men's hockey and blazing trails for women behind the bench.

- **Kendall Coyne Schofield** – Olympic medalist, NBC Sports broadcaster, and player development coach with the Chicago Blackhawks.

These women—and so many others—are shaping hockey's present and future.

In a world where women are often sidelined in sports narratives, Maddie's story is a small nod to the real pioneers breaking into front offices, challenging old systems, and proving that hockey is better when everyone is at the table.

xo

Cindy

CHAPTER

One

FEBRUARY 1995

MY FINGERS TRACED over the application packet. The Rhodes Scholarship. A prestigious award for academic excellence. Leadership. Character. Commitment to service.

Zero pressure.

For a second, I wondered why I'd even picked up the application. The University of Oxford was after geniuses or future prime ministers. People who ran nonprofits out of their dorm rooms, not mixed-race women from Cow Town. Even if they did happen to be excellent at math.

I flipped to the front page and started to read with my purple pen at the ready. International post-grad study. The idea sent tingles to my toes. While I'd at least crossed the Canadian border and even an ocean thanks to the trip to Hawaii I took with my mom last Christmas, I'd never travelled abroad. My mom had never travelled abroad. Quebec was the closest thing to European culture either of us had experienced, and I was itching to get out, and fall would be a perfect time.

I highlighted a few dates and application requirements, then set the packet down on my newly thrifted computer desk when I got to the section on extracurriculars. It was shocking how quickly my sense of self disintegrated with one bolded headline.

My grades were perfect. I was on the Dean's list. I'd just submitted a paper that made my differential equations professor raise both eyebrows and mutter, "Impressive." The best compliment I'd ever received from anyone in the math department. I'd done everything asked of me with flying colours, but leadership? Service? I wasn't exactly organizing protests or feeding the homeless. Unless you counted feeding Sharla and Crystal for three weeks last fall when they forgot to grocery shop.

I glanced at the little corkboard above my desk. Pinned to it was a faded postcard from Maui, a colour-coded study schedule for finals, and a photo of my mom and me from Christmas—both of us in leis, her arm around my shoulder. She'd cried when I told her I wanted to apply for grad school overseas. Not just because she didn't want me to go, but because there was no way in hell she could afford it. I'd paid my own way here at Douglas with scholarships and summer work. Without the Rhodes, we both knew this dream was dead in the water.

I reached for my pen again and tapped it against the corner of the pamphlet. *Get involved. Show initiative. Serve the community.* I had six months until I needed to submit. Six months to figure out how to pad my resume and—

A knock rapped on my half-closed bedroom door, followed by a creak as it swung wider. "Please tell me you're not double-checking your GPA calculation for fun again."

I looked up to see Tash standing there, one hand on her hip, the other holding a Diet Coke can with a blue-and-white-striped straw poking out. Her curly red hair was twisted up with a pencil, and she was wearing a Velvet Underground T-shirt that was technically mine.

I sighed. "Not for fun. For existential clarity."

She stepped inside, her toenails the colour of caution tape today. "You know what would give existential clarity . . . "

I grinned. "I'm not sleeping with Garrett."

Tash chortled and yelled out the door, "Sorry, G! It's a no again today!" She waited for the front door of the apartment to slam before flopping onto the bed.

Tash was an art history major and, after backpacking through Europe the previous summer, was convinced a study of emotionally repressed oil paintings was the only path to true enlightenment. Garrett was her best friend. Who also happened to have an enormous, very public crush on me. If he didn't smoke weed like it was his daily multivitamin, I might have been interested.

She reached out and plucked the Rhodes pamphlet from my desk. "Oh, we're in scholarship crisis mode. Excellent. Should I grab snacks or are we skipping straight to wine and despair?"

"Neither." I snatched it back. "I'm just considering my options."

"Babe, you have plenty of options that don't involve jumping through bureaucratic hoops."

I gave her a look. We'd had this conversation before. Tash insisted I only needed seven hundred dollars for a plane ticket and a good backpack to do all the studying in Europe I needed. I was convinced I'd be snatched and forced into sex trafficking if I spent the night at a hostel.

So, we were at an impasse.

I slumped down beside her, leaning back on the decorative pillows I'd had since I was fourteen. "You're connected to the world of social justice. Any causes I can start a rally for? A committee I can join?"

Tash snorted. "I hear the Manatees are having a moment."

I blinked. "Fighting for . . . their land rights?"

"They're sea creatures. Like whales, but cuter. Nipples in their fin crotch."

I made a face. "Doesn't sound like something I'd be into."

Tash dropped the packet. "What, fin-crotch nipples or saving sea creatures?"

I laughed. "Both. Either. Ugh. What am I going to do?"

"Easy. Just tell them the truth. You're a terrible person who doesn't care about anything besides algorithms and, oddly, minor league hockey."

I gasped. "Damn it, what time is it?" I leaned over Tash and scrambled for my watch. She snatched it off the nightstand and handed it to me.

6:44 p.m. The game started at seven. Which meant I was officially ten minutes behind my usual leaving time and twenty minutes behind Shar's. Luckily, she'd gone over to the rink early tonight with Rob, so I only had Crystal to disappoint.

I hopped off the bed with a hasty goodbye to Tash, grabbed my coat and keys, and half-ran, half-hopped down the apartment stairs like the floor was lava. Outside, the spring wind cut across the street, still carrying that icy edge that screamed "Remember, this is Alberta, don't get cocky." My poor Rabbit was parked under the same sad street lamp it always was, looking like it had just finished a twelve-round fight with a snowplow. To be fair, it probably had.

The driver-side mirror was still duct-taped, and the left headlight had flickered since February. I threw myself into the driver's seat, jammed the key into the ignition, and whispered a small prayer to the gods of German engineering. The engine sputtered, coughed, and finally choked awake.

"Thank you." I patted the cracked dashboard. "You're a queen. A temperamental, gas-guzzling queen." I tore away from the curb and headed toward Crystal's place, hitting every red light like it was some cosmic joke.

Crystal was waiting on the curb in her ridiculous fuzzy earmuffs and her scarf that matched mine, sipping a Slurpee like it was already July. I leaned over and flung the door open. "So sorry I'm late!"

She hopped in, and I peeled away from the curb as the door shut. The Rabbit whined but obeyed, bless her patchwork soul. We crested the hill leading to the rink, and I couldn't help but grin.

I loved these nights. Not just because Shar got aggressively into chirping at the other team's bench or because Crystal brought me snacks in her Mary Poppins bag of a purse. I loved them because hockey, in its own ridiculous, high-speed, sweaty way, made sense.

People thought math was rigid—just numbers, formulas, and logic. But good math? Real math? It was full of flow. Of momentum. Of elegant, precise chaos. Like a perfect pass sequence or a power play that snapped into place so cleanly it felt like watching a proof unfold across the ice.

Hockey was math in motion. Every breakout was a problem set. Every shift was a permutation of variables—angles, velocity, pressure, timing. There were infinite ways to get from puck drop to goal horn, but the most beautiful ones followed an internal rhythm. You could feel when it was right.

Players didn't realize they were doing math, but they were. Vectors. Trajectories. Instantaneous adjustments with spatial reasoning. The best players didn't just react. They anticipated. It was all there: the geometry of a tight-angle shot, the symmetry of a well-executed cycle, the algorithm of a three-on-two that ended with the goalie sprawled and hopeless.

It wasn't rigid. It was poetry. The only kind I could follow.

"Is Chase going to be there tonight?" Crystal asked.

A blush rose to my cheeks. "Uh . . . how would I know?"

Crystal raised an eyebrow, grinning. "All I have to do is say his name—"

"Stop. He's my stepbrother."

"*Was.* For what, a few months?"

Technically less. "Sorry, I didn't mean to snap."

"You definitely snapped."

"Yeah, well. The whole thing is just . . . weird. I don't know how to act around him. That's all this is." I gestured to my flushed neck.

"Uh-huh."

"Seriously."

"Dude, Chase is hot—"

"Can you not?"

"He's twenty-four, a hockey player, *graduated*."

I laughed and waved her off, trying to hide my reaction to the sudden swoop in my belly. I didn't know if Chase was objectively hot or not because to me, he was an icon. The symbol of everything I wanted and could never have in high school. His physical appearance back then was beside the point. It was the way he didn't seem to care. The way he moved. Fluid and almost lazy. The way he sprawled out in his chair. The way he always breathed out a little and dropped his eyes when he smiled. Like he was in on some secret joke that, at fourteen, I would've chopped off my left arm to hear.

Just the thought of him slipping his hand into the pocket of his faded jeans back then or leaning against his locker at school . . . All of that was why I reacted the way I did when my mom announced that her new boyfriend, the D-bag who always sat on our couch after school and waited for her to make him dinner, was Chase's dad.

Chase—the guy every girl swooned over at school. *His dad.*

I was a deer in headlights. At least fifteen seconds passed during which I wasn't sure if I'd gone into cardiac arrest. And the first time he stepped foot in my house? He probably thought I was mute. I don't think I said a word to him until he asked for help with his math when I wandered into the kitchen.

Math had been a mask to hide behind back then, but now? What was I supposed to do with all that? I wasn't in grade nine anymore, and yet the second he stood in front of me, I may as well have been sprouting breast buds and wearing braces. Which made no sense, considering all that coolness didn't seem to translate into anything impressive for Chase as an adult. He was back home coaching a hockey team. Like an ordinary person, not the demi-god I made him out to be.

I tuned back in to Crystal chatting about the after party at Ranchman's, trying to forget about running into Chase for the first time at Douglas near the washrooms, and nodded to show I was listening as I pulled into a parking spot at the back. Thankfully, the lot wasn't full despite our tardy arrival.

The hot dog and popcorn-laced air inside the arena hit us like a wall the second we pushed through the doors. Crystal pulled her earmuffs off with a dramatic flourish and tucked them into the pocket of her coat. The pink in her hair had faded from Barbie to Alberta rose. I'd always been a little jealous of her light hair. My hair was so dark, I'd have to bleach it to colour it. When I tried that in grade twelve, the ends of my curls had broken off. Not my best moment.

The arena wasn't packed, but the lower bleachers were full. Thankfully, Shar had already saved our seats. The student section was a mosaic of maroon and gold, and we spotted her waving at us from our usual spot—third row, just off centre ice, right behind the penalty box.

"Did we miss the goalie warm-ups?" Crystal craned her neck as we made our way to the stairs.

By the way our guys were already skating through drills, I was sure we had. A travesty. "Do you think we're bad people for objectifying them?" Thoughts like that were a dime a dozen in my brain. Most premises couldn't sit undisturbed for long, and this was one I revisited often. Would I be offended if men openly discussed watching female athletes gyrate their hips? Absolutely. Though I couldn't think of a sport where women were as fully clothed as hockey players. Except for, you know, actual women's hockey.

Crystal scoffed. "Pfft. No, we're not bad people. First of all, they're our friends, and I would say anything I think about their groin stretches straight to their faces. They'd think it was funny. Second, they're the ones fake-moaning when Tim goes spread-eagled."

That was a fair point.

Crystal paused on the stairs for a couple sitting on the aisle to stand, then slid in to sit next to Shar. I dropped onto the bench beside her.

"Who's going spread-eagled?" Shar shoved over a bag of popcorn.

"Your mom." Crystal grinned.

Shar ignored her, but the corner of her mouth lifted. "Okay, so they've got that massive defenceman—uh, Birkett?" She motioned to the Edmonton players running drills and pointed at number twenty-one. "Six-foot-four and made of cement blocks. Rob said he checked Bear into the boards so hard last year, they had to replace the glass." I winced. "Oh, and their goalie's new," Shar went on. "Transferred from U of S mid-season. Rob says he's good. Like, shutout-three-games-in-a-row good. But a total headcase if you rattle him early."

Crystal smirked. "Am I flashing him, or are you?"

I sighed. "If he saw my girls, he'd only be more amped up. Can't give them that advantage."

Shar laughed and reached for the popcorn, and the familiar ritual settled into my bones. Out on the ice, the teams were lining up for the anthem. The lights dimmed slightly, and after a brief introduction of the high school tenor from Airdrie, the first few notes of *O Canada* echoed through the rafters.

The kid was good. Not that I was a singer, but standing in front of an arena full of people to do anything that drew attention was impressive. Also my personal hell.

The arena burst into cheers and applause as the last notes reverberated, and the boys set up for their first shift. I leaned forward, elbows on my knees, frowning. Something was off. Was their starting lineup different tonight?

As my eyes swung to the bench, I froze. My mouth went dry. There he was. Back behind the Outlaws' bench. Leaning over the boards, arms crossed, mouth tight.

Chase.

Even though I'd seen him face-to-face the week prior, the sight of him made my stomach flip. Had he gotten a haircut since that night at Ranchman's? No, maybe it was that he hadn't shaved. That scruffy jaw thing he'd only barely pulled off at nineteen was now annoyingly, unfairly hot. He wore a black Outlaws jacket with the logo stitched over his heart, and when he shouted something to a player on the ice, I caught a brief clip of his voice.

My teenage golden calf.

Though Chase had been my stepbrother briefly in high school, we barely lived in the same house since he was constantly partying and sleeping over at his girlfriend's house. *Melody Sanchez.*

When I saw Chase at Ranchman's, I thought of her for the first time in probably five years. Later that night as I lay in bed, memories flaring to life, I remembered why I hated her so much.

That year was brutal. Mom and Dustin—Chase's dad— weren't getting along, and the walls in that house were thin enough to hear everything. Chase was seventeen and his mythic self. Always grabbing his hockey gear and disappearing out the front door if he deigned to appear at home in the first place.

I rarely initiated conversation with him at school, even though I watched his every move and thought about him more than what was probably healthy. But there was this one after- noon when we were both home, our parents still at work. I pumped myself up for a solid thirty minutes before gathering enough courage to ask if he'd take me to a book launch down- town the following day. It was stupid. Just a YA author I liked who was doing a signing at Chapters. But it felt monumental at the time. I didn't have friends who read like I did, and Mom was too wrapped up in work and her failing relationship to notice I hadn't left the house for anything that wasn't school in over a month.

Chase had looked up from tying his shoes and said, "Yeah. Sure. I'll drive you." He didn't even hesitate. I rode that high for a full twenty-four hours. Then, the next afternoon, I waited on the porch for forty-five minutes. In jeans I'd ironed. Lip gloss I'd borrowed. A copy of the book clutched so tightly, the pages curled.

I didn't think he'd be impressed or see me as anything but a dorky kid, but there was always a small part of me that hoped. That fantasized he'd look over at me and really see who I was.

That made his no-show cut even deeper.

I ended up walking to the corner store and buying a Coffee Crisp with my babysitting money. When I got home, he stood beside his car with Melody. She laughed at something he said in her cropped denim jacket and high ponytail. Chase had his hand on her waist, and she leaned in and kissed him. With tongue.

I hated her for that. For being cool and older and easy to want. I hated him more, but I didn't understand that yet.

The one-sided feud fizzled when he started needing math help. Easy to forget when he was paying attention to me. Then he left to play hockey, and I never saw him again. Our parents broke up, and that was that. It was water under the bridge, but it felt a little like self-betrayal that I was now sitting here ogling his forearms. Chase Wilson didn't care about me. He never had. He cared about his grades, his social life, and his hockey career. I needed to cut this weird obsession with him free once and for all.

But damn. Those forearms.

"I don't see Axel. Or Rory." Crystal squinted at the lineup as the puck dropped. "They're not starting?"

Right. That's what I'd been investigating. My attention snapped back to the ice. I was correct in thinking something was off. Number sixteen, Axel, and number five, Rory, the Outlaws' top forward line, weren't anywhere near the face-off circle.

Crystal's jaw dropped as we found them behind the bench without their gear on. "What the hell? Are they benched?"

Shar wet her lips. "Rob told me they aren't allowed to play until they get their grades back up."

I straightened, the words clicking through me like tumblers in a lock. "They were serious." It wasn't a question. Of course they were serious. This wasn't the United States, where the NCAA brought in TV spots or sponsorship money. Canadian universities prioritized academics, and they didn't give special privileges to student athletes.

While plenty of our friends on the Outlaws were hopeful they'd get a shot at a WHL or AHL tryout, those opportunities were rare. Though Logan had proven it wasn't impossible to get back in the running for pro consideration. He left only a few weeks into the semester to play for the Fredericton Canadiens and put his degree on hold.

A slow heat crept up the back of my neck as my brain revved. *I needed service hours.* I could offer to help them, but was tutoring athletes a thing? This couldn't be just an "Oh, I spend time volunteering at the animal shelter on weekends" kind of thing. I needed something official—something that looked impressive— to add to my application.

The first period dragged. Without Axel and Rory, the team lacked bite. If someone told me Edmonton had been on the power play for the first eight minutes, I would've believed them. We barely visited the neutral zone.

"Bear's already gassed," Shar muttered halfway through the second. "They're double-shifting him again."

The scoreboard reflected exactly what we were seeing on the ice. It was 2–0 for the Prairie Devils, and the crowd started feeling it. Less cheers, more groans. The guy beside me spilled half his nachos, yelling something about line changes, and even Crystal had stopped heckling.

By the time the third rolled around, it was painful. Edmonton scored again on a power play that left the Outlaws' defence hanging their heads. Rob was trying to rally the guys, but wasn't having much luck.

"They're unravelling," Crystal murmured.

She wasn't wrong. After losing Logan and now without Axel and Rory, there was no spark. No flow. Rob was stranded out there.

"What if I tutor them?" I pushed my curls behind my ears. Sharla and Crystal's eyes widened. "What? How bad could it be?"

"Babe, you don't exactly have a bunch of extra time." Crystal gave me a skeptical look.

"And have you met Axel and Rory?" Sharla added.

I held up a hand. "Okay, let me put it this way. I could look into tutoring them." My brain circled around the idea. It was a good option. Something I was already good at, something I felt passionate about. "I need service hours for my scholarship application, so maybe I can work something out with the coaches—"

"You mean with Chase?" Crystal raised an eyebrow, and the rest of that sentence died on my tongue. "He's the compliance coach. You'd have to coordinate with him on that, right?"

I cleared my throat. "I guess so. Probably."

Sharla jabbed Crystal playfully. "You aren't going to leave her alone about this, are you?"

Crystal laughed. "Nope. Not as long as she keeps blushing like that."

I rolled my eyes, immediately second-guessing myself. What if Oxford didn't care about student athletes? Did they even have hockey in England, or did they only play cricket and . . . football?

Wait—I was thinking about this all wrong. It wasn't Oxford who made the selections. It was the committee at Douglas, then the provincial committee. I'd read that somewhere in the packet. Hockey was a sure bet for them, wasn't it?

"I think it's a great idea." Sharla looped an arm over my shoulders. "I'm sure Rob would help make it happen if you want."

The Prairie Devils scored again, and a collective groan sounded throughout the arena. I clenched my fists with resolve. These guys were my friends, and I wouldn't let their season end like this. Plus, tutoring would be a win-win. Whatever weirdness I felt around Chase would have to take a backseat because this was the Rhodes freaking Scholarship.

And I was going to earn it.

CHAPTER

Two

MY PULSE SKIPPED as we descended the stairs to the concrete hall that led to the locker rooms. Sharla wanted to see Rob, obviously. The two of them had been attached at the hip since they got together, and while I was sometimes annoyed that Sharla wasn't spending as much time with us, I was truly happy for them.

It wasn't a surprise to me or Crystal that Rob had a thing for her. What had been surprising? That he'd won her over. Last semester, all she'd done was complain about him being in her and Logan's space. Although now that I thought about it, that should have been a red flag in and of itself. She always had strong feelings for him. And if the Buffy the Vampire Slayer film had taught me anything, it was that someone who annoyed you would probably be your love interest.

The Zamboni slid in lazy circles around the ice, erasing any sign of the game as we passed along the boards. We stopped at the benches lining the far wall. Sharla bounced on the balls of her feet, waiting for Rob. "I'm going to kill Axel and Rory," she muttered. "There's no way we should have lost to that team."

Crystal tucked a strand of her soft pink hair behind her ear. "It sucks."

I nodded. Rory and Axel liked to have a good time, no doubt about that. But I was surprised it had gotten so bad that they'd been benched.

Sharla shook her head. "I do see them studying when I'm over at the house. They don't seem like they're just slacking off. And I doubt they'd be putting on a good show for me."

A memory jumped to my mind unbidden—me leaning over Chase's math textbook, circling a sentence with my fingertip. "It's right here. The angles have to equal—"

"Yeah, I get that it's right there, but that doesn't mean I know when to use it."

"You just need more practice."

Chase ran a hand through his hair. "This makes sense to your brain, Maddie. I don't think with all the practice in the world, this is going to be simple for me."

That had been one of the first times I considered that maybe school didn't always get easier with hard work—that maybe I had a special capability. If I were honest, in that moment, I'd been judging Chase. Assuming he didn't want to try or put in the work. But then I'd seen Crystal struggle through entry-level chemistry. Her C+ wasn't from a lack of trying.

"It's not even that I want them to win all the time," Sharla continued. She leaned back against the painted cinder blocks. "This is their last couple of years of competitive hockey. It's hard enough to go through Juniors and not make it into the higher leagues. But then to come to college and not even be able to play . . ."

I nodded. "More than that. What are they going to do after this?" There was always a chance that one of them got into a feeder league or went over to play in Europe or something. Logan was proof of that. But the majority of these guys were going to have to rely on the degree they earned to get a regular job.

The door to the locker room banged open, and Axel and Rory exited first. It made sense since they didn't even have to shower or change. Rory's expression was clouded over, and Axel hung his head.

"Hey, guys." Crystal gave a smile that looked more like a wince. Rory lifted his hand in a small wave. They started to walk past, obviously not in the mood for conversation, but I reached out and grabbed Axel's arm.

"Hey, can I ask you something?"

He exhaled, his jaw tight. "Sure. What's up?"

I dropped my hand and took a step back. I always forgot how tall Axel was until he was standing in front of me. "I want to help. With your grades."

Axel glanced at Rory, then turned his attention back to me. "We just haven't had as much time to study because of these extra practices."

My eyes narrowed. "What extra practices?"

Rory and Axel exchanged another look.

Sharla exhaled. "Did Rob rope you guys into that? He told me he was doing it on his own."

"Rob's been doing extra practices?" Crystal asked.

She nodded. "I guess a scout is coming in April—"

"Coach Wilson has a connection."

I blinked. Coach Wilson. That was Chase's last name. *He had a connection with a hockey scout?* So it was what I thought. Logan had gotten an opportunity with the AHL, and now the rest of the team was ready to shoot their shot. I couldn't blame them for it, but I wasn't exactly the right person to talk to about dreaming. Following the rules of societal engagement and working my ass off had always gotten me more than fantasizing.

I straightened. "Okay. That's great if you want to do extra practices, but you can't let everything slip, or you'll lose time on the ice." I put my hand on my hip. "I hate to go all maternal on you, but what will you do if you fail out of Douglas and don't get a spot on a feeder team?" I wasn't going to quote the stats for them. I'd save that for later if they chose to be difficult.

Rory shrugged. "Their expectations are too high. It's not like I'm failing."

"What are their requirements?"

"We have to have at least a B in every class." Rory looked scandalized.

"And you currently have—"

"A's and B's. And . . . two barely C's."

I considered that for a moment. "Okay. That's not bad at all. We can totally work with that. Which classes?"

"Applied math and bio."

"Easy. What about you?"

Axel's lips pulled into a thin line. "I've got two C's, in Calc and one of my engineering classes." He paused a moment. "And one D." His voice was so low I could barely distinguish the words.

I tried not to make him feel more ashamed than he already was. "Which class is that in?"

"Art history."

I pursed my lips to keep from smiling. "You signed up for art history?"

"It was one of the options," he mumbled.

"Okay." I analyzed the next steps. I could just schedule a time with them to study, but that wouldn't work for me. I needed this to be on the books. "I'll help you guys, and I know we can get your grades up if you're willing to work. But I think if you talk with your professors and coaches, we could set something up so you don't have to miss any practices or game—"

"There's no way Coach Wilson will do that," Axel cut in. "He's a hard-ass."

I worked to mask my surprise. *Chase was a hard-ass?* That was the funniest thing I'd heard all week. Chase Wilson was the kid who hit the record for most classes ditched in grade eleven, and he didn't have grade twelve to outdo himself because he was long gone by then. I didn't even know if he finished high school, though it didn't matter if he'd graduated with his bachelor's degree.

I nodded. "I'll talk to him. See what we can figure out."

Rory's face lit up. "Maddie girl." He moved in for a hug, throwing his arms around me. "You're the best."

I had to admit. Hugs from guys on the Outlaws hockey team felt like snuggling in a warm blanket, and I didn't hate it. It wasn't until they'd started up the stairs that I realized what I'd agreed to.

I was going to have to talk to Chase again.

———

I stood in the hall the next morning outside of the small office next to the weight room on the main floor of the ice arena, now dubbed the Douglas Dome since they refinished the roof last month. The name seemed to be starting to catch on.

I took weight lifting my freshman year and learned how to do real squats for the first time. Something I should've taken more seriously in high school when I was actually playing sports.

I wasn't sure if Chase—*Coach Wilson. Damn it, I was going to have to get used to that*—was in this office, but it was my best guess. Also safer than running into him after a game or practice or something where the other players would see us. Or where I might be too casual like I'd been at Ranchman's and blurt out how I used to have a crush on him in high school. Not my best moment.

I closed my eyes and inhaled through my nose. It didn't matter. That was then, this was now, and there was no reason to be on edge. All of the things that were thigh-achingly attractive to me when I was fourteen didn't hold water now. Back then, I wanted cool. But these days? I wanted driven. Smart. Financially secure. Chase and I were on different paths, and I could hold my own.

I straightened and walked forward, pushing through the door and stepping into the small reception area. A woman with a grey bob and glasses looked up. "Can I help you?"

I smiled. "I need to speak with Coach Wilson. It's about a compliance issue for the Outlaws."

The receptionist nodded, then stood from her chair with a squeak. Her skirt stretched over her hips and the slit showed the tops of her knee high socks. My heart thudded as she rounded the corner and disappeared from view. Suddenly, the idea of seeing Chase—of showing up here unannounced—seemed like the worst error in judgment. I could've sent him an email. I could've met with Coach Blakely instead of—

"He's out for lunch, can I leave him a message?" The receptionist had reappeared in front of me without me noticing.

"Mmhm. Sure." I waited for her to pull out a pad of paper and a pen. "I'm Madelyn Taylor." I gave my full name. Seemed more professional. Less like I'd ogled sixteen-year-old Coach Wilson as he exited my washroom in only a towel. "I wanted to discuss a tutoring program for the players who—"

"Tutoring?"

I spun at the sound of a male voice behind me. A male voice I recognized. Chase stood there, leaning against the open office door, his hand wrapped around the handle.

CHAPTER

Three

HOW HAD *I not heard the door open?*

"Hey, Maddie." He breathed out a little and dropped his eyes as he smiled. He wore an Oxford shirt and khakis. Very professional. Very un-Chase.

I couldn't stop staring at his mustache. "Uh, hey." I glanced back at the receptionist, who was wadding up the note she'd just started. "Yes. I stopped by because I heard some of the guys were benched due to their grades."

"You were serious then?" he asked, and I frowned. He strode toward the counter and let the door swing closed behind him. The reception area was small to begin with, and now it felt like curbside at a Canada Day parade. "When you said to phone you if I needed math help."

My mouth opened and closed. Ranchman's. When I ran into him by the washrooms. I'd been trying to play it cool. *Had I really said that?* "I guess I was." The receptionist sat behind the desk, watching us.

Chase nodded. "I'll keep that in mind." He shoved a hand in his pocket, and I seriously started wondering if he was pulling out all his old moves on purpose. Then I realized what an idiot I was because these weren't moves. They were . . . normal signs of human existence.

"Okay, yeah. But I was wondering—I'm thinking about applying for the Rhodes Scholarship." *Thinking? I wasn't thinking about it, I was definitely applying. Why had I said it like that?* "I'm looking for opportunities to serve Douglas and the community, and I figured this was a problem close to home that I could help solve. I'd love to talk with you about setting up—"

"I've got some things in the works already. But I appreciate you offering." Chase leaned over the counter and said something to the receptionist that I couldn't hear with all the blood rushing in my ears.

Was he dismissing me? Not even considering what I had to say? What, he was a few years older than me and had on a pressed, collared shirt, and suddenly he was the expert? Maybe he'd been trained in coaching, and he definitely knew hockey better than I did, but between the two of us, I could guarantee I had the upper hand when it came to studying, test-taking, and good grades.

"What are they?" I folded my arms over my chest.

Chase turned his head. "Hm?"

"Your 'things in the works.' What are they?" I took a step closer and cleared my throat. "I'm here offering my services and—"

"You have services?" The corner of his mouth twitched.

Oh, he was making me see red. "Yes. Tutoring services." I scrambled for data to corroborate the claim I was about to make. I'd helped Crystal with her bio class after she'd struggled so hard with chem. I'd worked with Tash in her ecology class, and both had pulled out B's. That was a hundred percent track record as far as I was concerned. "I guarantee at least B grades with all of the students I mentor, and I believe that's what your players need to remain in good standing." That was excellent—professional, concise. I gave myself a mental pat on the back.

"Are you sure that's a promise you can make? You've never

had a student who didn't pass that mark?" His eyes glinted, and heat rose to my cheeks. I was back in the kitchen, watching him tap his pencil eraser on the strip of blank paper at the top of his Math 20 test. I could still see the streaks of red slashing through half of the numbered questions.

I wet my lips. "Only one. And I learned from it."

Chase held my gaze, and the temperature in the room seemed to rise a few degrees. I flinched when he dropped his hand on the countertop. "I've got a meeting I need to get to, but I'll reach out."

Hope warred with annoyance in my chest. Had I done enough to convince him? But also, why had I needed to convince him? He, of all people, knew what I was capable of. "Sure. I can give you my number. It's the one I share—"

"Oh, I can access your student email."

I paused with my hand reaching over the counter for a pen. Right. He was a staff member. He could see my entire file if he wanted to. So embarrassing. "Right. Okay. Thank you." I spun on my heel and walked to the door.

"Taylor, right?" Chase asked. "That's your last name? So I can look it up."

I turned back, my jaw set. *What the hell?* Was he messing with me on purpose? Or . . . had he really forgotten my personal details?

This had to be a joke. Or a messed-up power play. He'd lived in my house. Sat in my kitchen. He'd been the one to say hi at Ranchman's, and now he was pretending he didn't know my last name? "You got it," I snapped, then threw the door open and strode into the hall.

———

Chase didn't reach out.

The rest of the week, I checked my email in the library first thing when I arrived on campus, then before I left to go home for the evening. Nothing. By Friday, I was about ready to march back over to the ice arena and light into him, but my pride—and the rational side of me that knew if I was caught cussing out a member of administration it wouldn't look good on my student record—kept me on the south side of campus.

I breezed into the coffee shop and sat at our usual table. It was the kind of place that promised flaky croissants but delivered scones that could chip teeth. Still, we loved it—mostly for the crooked tables and the barista with the Morrissey tattoo who let Crystal play her mixtapes on the speakers when it wasn't busy.

Shar passed me my drink, and I stirred it with the included wooden stick, aggressively not checking the time. Or thinking about the fact that I hadn't been to the library that morning to check my email.

Crystal raised an eyebrow as she peeled the wrapper off a blueberry muffin. "You going to admit you're spiralling, or do we need to have an intervention?"

I raised an eyebrow. "What do you call this?"

"A logistical question." Shar sipped her drink. "You're acting weird."

"I am not." I reached out and pulled a piece from Crystal's muffin.

"Is this about the tutoring?" Shar asked.

I avoided their eyes. "What tutoring?" It was stupid. I should've admitted it right away. I should've told them what happened with Chase the second I left that office, but something had held me back. I'd hoped to talk with them about it after I got an email in my inbox. After I'd set something up so I had some kind of success to report.

"Yep. Bullseye." Crystal leaned back in her chair.

"I'm sorry." I slumped over the table, pushing my curls out of my face. "I didn't mean to shut down."

Shar put a hand on my arm. "After two years, we kind of know how you work."

I gave her a skeptical look. "How is that?"

She grinned. "Late night talks. That's when you open up."

"We've all been so busy, we didn't realize we needed a girls' night. Buuuut." Crystal's eyes lit up as she straightened in her chair. "That's changing tonight. We're going out."

The tension that had been coiled inside me all week released a little. "Yes. That's exactly what I need." No more obsessing about transcripts or resume padding, no more waiting for my email to load. "Where are we going?"

"Trivia night at the Den." Crystal threw her hands up, sending muffin crumbs off the edge of the table.

I laughed out loud. "Because you want to win another twenty percent off coupon at Boston Pizza?"

"I heard they're giving out free zoo tickets!" Crystal's eyes glittered, and I couldn't help but feel flattered. The last time we'd gone to the Den at the University of Calgary for trivia night, we'd beaten every other team by a minute and a half on our response time and got every question right. Well, I got every question right.

"Rob's okay with this?"

Shar nodded resolutely. "Yep. He's doing an extra practice, and I told him to stay as late as he wanted at the rink."

Crystal grinned. "I love that his hockey dreams give us more of you."

Shar laughed, shoved the last of her muffin into her mouth, and stood. "Alright. I need to warm up before my solo audition."

I pushed back from the table. "And I've got Complex Variables."

Crystal shook her head. "You shouldn't look happy about that statement."

I grabbed my bag and slung it over my shoulder. "Pick you up tonight?"

I MADE it to the science theatre with three minutes to spare, winded from speed-walking across campus and dodging two separate high school tour groups and a guy trying to sell student union planners out of a duffel bag.

The class was already half full. Turns out, math students are huge nerds and have nothing better to do than show up early to lecture. Professor Kowalski stood at the front, fiddling with the transparency projector. He wore his usual tweed jacket and brown slacks, his salt and pepper hair tufting in the back like a duckling.

He looked up as I slid into my usual seat near the front. "Miss Taylor." *See? He hadn't been to my house or walked down my hall half naked, and he still remembered my last name.* "A word, if you've got a second before we start?"

My pulse kicked up. Not because I was in trouble—Kowalski liked me—but because being summoned by an authority figure still triggered academic fight-or-flight in my DNA. I stood and walked down to the front, clutching my notebook like a shield.

"A little bird told me that you recently offered to tutor a couple of student-athletes." He ground the R's in that sentence, his eastern European accent mostly beaten out of him after living in Alberta for the past forty years.

My spine straightened. A little bird? The only person who knew I'd offered tutoring was Chase. Warmth bloomed in my chest. Had he been talking about me to other professors? "Yes? I mean—I offered, but I don't know if they're taking me up on it."

He tilted his head. "Well, I hope they do because, frankly, we need more students like you involved in the mess that is athletics right now."

Mess? He spat the words with enough passion that I almost believed he cared about something other than differential equations.

He adjusted his glasses. "Douglas is putting together a small academic-athletic oversight committee. It's in partnership with the registrar's office. We're looking at building a pilot program to support at-risk athletes academically." He muttered something under his breath, shook his head, and then the dam broke. "This is exactly the problem, Madelyn. We've got administrators bending over backward to keep players eligible like we're running some junior version of the NCAA. It used to be that if you couldn't keep up academically, you didn't play. Simple. Consequence. Accountability. But now? Now we're talking about 'retention support' and 'performance optimization' like these kids are fragile little glass dolls who'll break if they open a textbook."

He was heating up now, pacing a few steps in front of the projector cart. "You know what this is? It's American rot. That's what it is. Booster culture. Grade inflation. God help us, there's talk of corporate sponsorship on jerseys next year. Jerseys! Can you imagine? 'Douglas Outlaws brought to you by Tim Hortons.'"

He snapped a cap back on his pen like he was sealing a bomb. "This is academia, not a farm team. We're supposed to educate these students, not groom them for TSN highlight reels. But no—now we need committees to make sure our delicate athletes don't fall behind while they're off skipping class for a game in Moose Jaw."

He stopped suddenly, narrowed his eyes at a speck on the transparency, and scraped it off with his thumbnail. Then, like nothing had happened, he straightened. "I'd like you on it."

I blinked, trying to rewind and remember what we were talking about before the decline of University athletics. "On the committee?"

"You'd be the only student," he said. "Everyone else will be staff or faculty. It's not a casual ask."

"No, I—yes. I mean, absolutely. Yes."

Kowalski nodded once, satisfied. "Perfect. The first meeting is this afternoon. Four o'clock sharp."

Well. Nothing like spur of the moment. I tried to play it cool. But inside, I was already writing the scholarship essay paragraph in my head. *Demonstrated leadership and creative initiative in a revolutionary collaboration with administration for the support of student athletes—*

"Miss Taylor?"

My head snapped up.

Professor Kowalski looked amused. "I'd like to begin class now if it's alright with you."

"Yes. Of course. Sorry. And thank you so much for thinking of me."

He nodded once and turned to the projector as I found my seat. Four o'clock. That was fine. I would have just enough time to drive back to my apartment and change for trivia night, then come back for the meeting. That would save me the drive back again to pick up Shar and Crystal.

I pulled out my text, notebook, and pencil. So. Chase may not have emailed me, but obviously he'd been working behind the scenes. Did he know that something like this would be far more impressive than a simple paragraph about tutoring?

I grinned to myself, then turned my attention to the projector.

———

When my last class ended, I jogged to the parking lot and headed home, ignoring the way my Rabbit made a grinding noise every time I turned left. I would have exactly forty-three minutes to shower, change, and emotionally prepare myself for a faculty-led committee meeting. Kowalski had given me his thoughts on the athlete/academic situation, but I was beyond curious about what the other administrators and professors would bring to the table. Why would they start a committee if they didn't want to help? And why was the situation dire enough to require this kind of organization?

By the time I slammed the apartment door behind me, I'd already stripped off my jacket and pulled the scrunchie out of my hair. Tash looked up from her perch on the couch, a half-painted toe propped on the coffee table and a European cinema book open on her lap like Sailor Moon reruns weren't playing on the TV behind her on loop.

"Hot guy or crisis?" She raised one perfectly sculpted brow. "Never mind. A hot guy would be a crisis for you."

I snorted, kicking off my shoes and heading toward my room. "Trivia at the Den. Want to come?"

"To celebrate intellectual hedonism?"

"So that's a no?" I called over my shoulder. I darted into my room, yanked open my closet, and stared, faced with an instant conundrum. I pulled out my satin halter top. Definitely not appropriate for a committee meeting, but perfect for trivia night. I flicked through my blouses.

Tash appeared in the doorway. "Do you want to look like a librarian at trivia night?"

"Librarians here are all white."

Tash chortled. "You like math. You're the whitest girl I know."

I channelled all my attitude and flipped her the bird, but she wasn't wrong. Not having my dad around meant I grew up solely with my mom and her side of the family. As a kid, it wasn't until someone tried to touch my hair that I remembered I didn't look like everyone else.

Tash smirked and sat on my bed. She pointed at a black tank top—scoop-necked, fitted. "Your boobs look great in that."

"I can't wear that to my meeting."

"You said trivia night."

"Yeah. I have a meeting first, though." I frowned at a floral top I thought I'd thrown out last semester. It made me look like a kindergartner.

"So what you do is . . ." Tash jumped up and walked over to the closet. She grabbed a maroon knit sweater from the shelf and handed it to me. "Layer."

It was excellent advice. As long as the sweater didn't leave threads all over the tank top. I took a lint brush just in case.

I pulled into the university lot with time to spare but zero idea where I was going. The Douglas administration building loomed in front of me. I hadn't thought to ask Kowalski where the meeting was, but the offices were still open for the day. If I was in the wrong place, they'd be able to direct me. I leaned over to see myself in the rearview mirror and swiped on a layer of berry lipstick. Too much? Maybe. I tried not to overthink it.

I tucked the lipstick back in my coat pocket, grabbed my bag, and opened the door. A blast of wind hit me square in the face, and I immediately regretted my shoe choice. Black heels under my bootcut jeans. Cute. Professional. Zero traction. Hopefully I wouldn't have to hike across campus.

I trudged up the walkway, dodging a sandwich wrapper that flung itself at my knee like a tiny paper ghost.

I burst through the doors and took a moment to compose myself in the airlock, then stepped inside. I walked up to the front desk, trying to ignore that the sharp click of my heels on the tile echoed through the entire atrium.

I smiled at the receptionist. "Hi, I'm here for the committee meeting?" I winced at the vagueness of that description. This was a university. They probably had more than a handful of committee meetings happening every afternoon.

"Madelyn Taylor?" She gave me a questioning look. When I nodded, she pointed me toward a sign that read, *Meeting Rooms A–D.* "You'll be in C."

I thanked her, then walked past the desk and down the hall. I'd never been past the entry of the admin building, and it felt strange. Privileged. Like I was seeing behind the scenes at Disney World.

I didn't have to do any sleuthing to find the room because Professor Kowalksi was standing at the end of the hall with a woman I didn't recognize. She had jet black hair that grazed her shoulders and an easy smile that made me wonder if she taught poetry or drama.

Kowalski introduced me—she was the Dean of Business, which made me internally promise that I would never make snap judgments about anyone again.

A promise which I immediately broke. Because as I walked into the room, after noticing that the walls were the colour of manila folders and there was a long, rectangular table that looked like it had been repurposed from a church basement, my eyes landed on a familiar figure.

He was at the far end of the table, seated sideways with one arm draped across the back of his chair, talking with someone. Chase looked up mid-sentence and froze, two lines forming between his brows.

He hadn't known I was coming. No, more than that. He had no idea it was a possibility that I would come. Which meant he hadn't been the little bird that talked with Kowalski. He hadn't emailed me, and he clearly hadn't done a damn thing to move forward with my tutoring offer.

Judgment snapped into place faster than a slapshot off the tape—clean, fast, and final. I didn't know anything about Chase Wilson. And I no longer wanted to.

CHAPTER
Five

CHASE BLINKED ONCE, then leaned back in his chair like nothing about my arrival rattled him, but it was too late. I'd already seen the evidence.

A man near the whiteboard turned around. "Ah, Madelyn Taylor, correct?"

I nodded, clutching the strap of my bag.

"Glad you could join us," he said warmly. "We were just getting started. I'm Dr. Howard Lamont. Vice Dean of Student Affairs. Thank you for coming in."

He gestured to a chair next to Chase as the others filtered into the room. Fantastic.

"Hey, Maddie—"

"Madelyn," I snapped before Chase could get the rest of that statement out. If he didn't want to remember anything? Fine. I could play that game, too.

I kept my body turned away from him as Dr. Lamont facilitated introductions. There were seven of us in total. Dr. Lamont, who looked a little like a youth pastor, Professor Kowalski, and Marcia Toews, a student support specialist with a high ponytail, very pink nails, and a soft smile. Then there was Coach Bryan from the women's volleyball team, who sat flipping his pen between his fingers; April Martin, the Dean of Business, whom I'd met in the hall; and Chase, who, even in my peripheral vision, looked irritatingly attractive in an Outlaws quarter-zip.

Dr. Lamont cleared his throat. "Now that everyone's here, let's start with the basics. This committee was formed in response to a growing concern from the registrar's office. Specifically, student-athletes falling short academically and the lack of sustainable structures to help them recover before it's too late."

Marcia nodded. "We've seen an increase in mid-season academic suspensions, especially among first- and second-year players."

"And," Kowalski added dryly, "an increase in excuses, extensions, and emails written by coaches instead of students."

Coach Bryan exhaled. "Listen, we're expecting these students to perform two jobs at once. We can't expect them to make both things their number one priority."

"It shouldn't even be a question," Kowalski rebutted. "None of these students are going to play professionally—"

"That's not true." Chase leaned over the table. "One of our players, as you know, had the opportunity to go to Juniors and is now out in Fredericton. I'm all for high academic expectations, but we're doing these students a disservice if we don't foster athletic potential."

"I agree." Coach Bryan nodded. "I think they need more support, and not because we're babying them." He held up a hand to stem what was sure to be an argument by Kowalski.

"If we want this to succeed, we have to be honest about the optics." April crossed one leg over the other, smoothing her pencil skirt. "This isn't just about helping students pass their classes—it's about creating a framework that feels credible to faculty, scalable for administration, and legitimate to the athletes themselves.

"Support is only effective if it's paired with standards. The second it feels like special treatment, you lose the academic side of the room. And the second it feels like punishment, the players disengage. You've got to sell the idea that academic performance is part of their brand as student-athletes—part of the deal they signed up for."

Damn. As I worked to pick apart all the facets of that comment, Lamont turned to me. "You're probably wondering why you're here."

No, I wasn't wondering. I'd assumed since my GPA had to be one of the highest on campus, and because I'd already offered to help with student athletes, I was there to offer a student perspective on success. The piece that didn't make sense was that I didn't play a sport here at Douglas. "Actually, I was wondering why you chose me instead of a high-performing student athlete." There had to be plenty of them. Wouldn't they have a better perspective on this topic?

"That's a great question." Lamont's eyes flicked to Kowalski. "We discussed different possibilities and decided it would be best not to add more to our athletes' plates. And some of us preferred inviting a student who prioritized academics over other pursuits."

Ah. So Kowalski put up a fuss about having an athlete here. Got it. I was still dying to know how he'd heard about my tutoring offer.

"This committee's goal is to create a pilot program for compliance and student athlete support," Lamont continued. "And as Coach Wilson already touched on, we have a situation with the men's hockey team that seems ripe for attention. So, we'd like to brainstorm together and start with one team–Outlaws hockey. If the program works, we scale to other sports."

Coach Bryan exhaled in relief.

I perked up. That was perfect. But, I reminded myself, this wasn't only about getting Rory and Axel back out on the ice. My interest was piqued. Could there be a way to help student athletes excel in both their sport and academics? Could we optimize their experience to maximize potential on either side? What were the factors that impacted their ability to perform? Time, obviously. Physical stamina. We didn't have control over their diet, genetics, or—

"Is that acceptable to you, Miss Taylor?"

I looked up. Everyone at the table had their eyes trained on me. I pursed my lips as my cheeks flushed with heat. "Sorry, I was thinking. I missed the question."

Mr. Lamont smiled. "I was suggesting that, as our student liaison and with your offer to provide tutoring hours, you meet directly with Coach Wilson to create a plan for the at-risk players on the Outlaws team. We'll continue to meet as a group as well. You two can report on what's working and what's not, and we'll collaborate. Does that work?"

It took everything in me not to reply with something like, "I think Coach Wilson already has some plans in the works," or, "That depends on whether Coach Wilson knows how to use his email." I gripped the edge of my seat and said, "I'd be happy to."

The meeting dragged on for another fifteen minutes, outlining progress metrics, shared calendars, then devolved when the subject of playing privileges was breached. Chase and I were assigned to present an initial schedule and proposed expectations by Monday in order to reach a consensus and implement the strategy before the next home game. So much for my sleepy weekend.

I succeeded in keeping the knowledge that I'd be meeting with Chase at surface level. It would be fine. Professional. Since he didn't think we had any kind of relationship anyway, it would be easy to keep our conversations focused. He was a different person now, and so was I. I could compartmentalize old Chase. Seal him up in a little box I could pull out every once in a while to admire when we weren't working on a project together. If I could do it with my past boyfriends, I could do it with an old high school crush.

It was past five when Lamont finally stood to dismiss us. I needed to bolt to get over to Crystal's place and then Shar's on time for trivia at six. I grabbed my bag and stood too fast, my thighs catching the bottom of the table as my chair legs caught on the carpet.

I winced, then smiled and thanked Lamont and Kowalski for the invitation, then slid past the others who were still seated and swept out of the room. My heel clicks felt even more abrasive now that the building was completely empty. The receptionist no longer sat at the desk, but thankfully, I had no trouble exiting through the locked doors.

I wrapped my arms around myself against the wind and hurried to the car. I yanked open the driver's door of the Rabbit and tossed my bag into the passenger seat with enough force to knock over an old coffee cup. Empty, thankfully.

I slid into the seat, shoved the key into the ignition, and turned.

Click.

I paused, then tried again.

Click.

I groaned, dropping my forehead to the steering wheel. Why? The building was closed, so I had no way to phone Crystal or Shar. Not unless I wanted to walk back up there and press myself to the glass in the hope that someone from the committee walked past and took pity on me.

"Come on," I muttered, turning the key again. And again.

Then a knock on the window nearly sent my soul into orbit. I shot up with a gasp to find Chase standing next to the car, hands in his coat pockets, the collar of his shirt popped up against the wind like he was starring in some CBC cop drama. His brows lifted. A silent question.

I cracked the door open. "It's fine. Just needs a minute."

He leaned down slightly. "I heard it clicking."

"Yeah. It does that sometimes." That was a lie. This had never happened before. Well, not since grade twelve when my mom had to drive me to school for a week. Our next-door neighbour had somehow fixed it over the weekend, and it had been fine ever since.

Chase stepped back, scanning the car. "Is this the same car you had in high school?"

"Hilarious." I pushed the door open further and stood. Chase frowned. "You can remember what car I drove, but not my last name?"

His nostrils flared. "It's not that I didn't remember your last name—"

"Then why did you ask?"

"I don't know, I wasn't sure if—maybe it had changed."

I gave him a look. "Changed? How?"

He shook his head and stalked to the back of the car. "Maybe your mom got remarried. Or . . . maybe you did."

I laughed out loud. "First of all, I wouldn't take any random guy's name if my mom remarried, and second, *you thought I was married?*"

Chase kicked one of the back tires and nodded to my hand. "You wear that ring."

My mouth opened, then snapped closed as I glanced down and saw the thin gold band around my ring finger. On my left hand. "Oh, no. That's—it was my dad's." I swallowed the guilt welling in my chest. Okay, so he had a good reason for asking about my last name.

I'd worn that band for so long, I didn't notice it anymore. Did other guys look at that and think I was married? Engaged? Was that why I never got hit on as much as Crystal and Shar? My entire university career suddenly flashed through my mind's eye.

Chase strode past me and opened the driver's side door, popping the hood. "How are you even driving this thing?"

"It works fine."

"It's an accident waiting to happen."

I rolled my eyes and walked closer to where he bent over the engine. There was barely enough light from the street lamp to see anything. "I don't take it far, just from my apartment to campus."

"How far is that?" He tinkered with something, then moved to wipe his fingers on his khakis and thought better of it.

"Twenty minutes. Ish."

He gave me a look, then shifted so he wasn't creating a shadow over the car's innards. "So your dad left and you still wear his ring?"

The question was a gut punch. All the air left my lungs, and I put out a hand to brace myself against the car.

Chase looked up. "What?"

"Is that what you thought?" I asked. He frowned. *So classic.* "My mom dated a black guy, got knocked up, and we never saw him again?"

"No, I—"

"My dad died. Heart attack. When I was six years old. So yes, I still wear his ring." I twisted the cool metal around my finger.

I didn't know where he got it. My mom didn't either. I found it when we were going through his things after the funeral, and I had to wait until I was twelve before it fit me. First, I'd worn it on my thumb. Then my middle finger. Finally, my ring finger on my left hand when I hit sixteen. It didn't fit as well on my right hand.

Silence.

Finally Chase said, "I'm so sorry. I didn't know."

"Yeah, well." I dropped my eyes. "You didn't ask."

Another long pause.

"It's probably the solenoid." Chase cleared his throat. "Happens in these older VWs. Ignition signal's weak, doesn't trigger the starter properly."

I lifted my head. Chase pulled his keys from his pocket, chose one, then fiddled for twenty seconds. "Try it."

I hesitated, then rounded the car door and sat. "Are you going to move your arm?"

He shook his head. "Just turn the key."

I did as he asked. The engine choked, then roared to life.

I stared at the dash. "You've got to be kidding me."

Chase lowered the hood and let it fall with a satisfying thunk. "German engineering. Terrible with cold starts. Worse with age."

I got out slowly, the wind yanking at my curls. "You know cars?"

Chase ignored the question. "You've got cracked vacuum hoses and your windshield wipers are on backwards."

"They still work." I pursed my lips, not wanting to mention the blinker.

He stepped closer. "Yeah, for now. But if one of those lines goes and your engine floods, you'll be stranded on Crowchild Trail with semis blasting past you."

"I don't drive on Crowchild."

"So you live west of campus?"

My insides flipped positions. When had he moved so close? I gripped the top of the door, my pulse jolting at my throat. "I have to go." Chase nodded and stepped back. "Thank you." I dropped into the driver's seat and closed the door, then reversed as Chase walked to the curb. He crouched and wiped his hand in the grass.

I took a shaky breath and drove to the exit.

CHAPTER
Six

THE DEN WAS ALREADY PACKED by the time we got there—shoulder to shoulder with undergrads, grad students, and a few profs pretending they weren't too old to be there. The scent of greasy onion rings and spilled Kokanee flooded my senses. String lights dangled low over sticky tables, and the guy on the mic was trying to be funny between questions, but the sound system cut out every third word. I might've been the only one who thought it was a fun exercise to try to decipher his code.

Crystal grabbed an answer sheet and a pencil then shoved past a table full of econ guys to reach our seats in the back, her pink hair bouncing with every step. "If we don't win tonight, I'm blaming the reverb." She dropped onto the bench across from me and immediately dug into the chili fries that the waiter had dropped off moments before.

Sharla tossed her short, dark bob out of her eyes and unzipped her fitted hoodie with flair. "I swear they changed their chili recipe. It used to have more kick."

I laughed. "Maybe you've acquired a tolerance." Sharla shrugged, then hopped up and switched sides of the booth, creating a two-on-one situation, and my face scrunched. "I don't even get a warm-up period?"

Sharla shook her head. "Nope. Spill."

The mic screeched, and the host barked, "Round one! Canadian history!"

Crystal smoothed the answer sheet and brandished the pencil. "We can do both."

I nodded, swallowing hard. "Okay, so, you know I was going to offer to tutor Axel and Rory?" Their heads bobbed like baby birds. "Well, I went to Chase and—"

"Which Canadian Prime Minister served the shortest term?" the host barked. It sounded more like "Which Can— ime— inister— served th— ortest ter—?"

I answered without hesitation. "Charles Tupper. Sixty-nine days."

Crystal stared at me, then scratched the answer on the sheet as I continued.

"I offered to help, Chase made it weird—"

"Weird, how?" Sharla pushed her hair behind her ears.

"I don't know? He asked what my last name was, and at first I thought he was just being an ass, but then when he was fixing my car—"

"He fixed your car?" Crystal's eyes were wide.

I blew out a breath and started in chronological order. I told them about the brief meeting with Chase in his office, the invitation from my math professor, the first committee meeting that evening, and the excitement with my Rabbit and Chase in the parking lot—all while throwing out answers about our great nation's history.

"That all happened this week?" Sharla flattened her back against the bench.

"Mostly today." I sighed. "Here's the thing. There's this—I don't know, this—"

"Sexual tension?" Crystal raised an eyebrow.

I shook my head. "No, it's not that." She gave me another look, and I scoffed, "I get that Chase is hot, okay? Yes, I find him attractive. What girl wouldn't? But it's not that. He's like—I don't know, even when he was living with us, there was some-thing—" I stopped mid-sentence.

Our waiter came to the table to collect our answer sheet and handed us a new one as the host announced the next subject. Movie quotes.

I barely noticed. "He's a puzzle," I murmured.

"Hm?" Sharla leaned in.

I looked between the two of them. "That's what it is. Chase has never made sense. He's a puzzle I can't figure out, and that doesn't happen to me." That's exactly what it was. He always acted so cool, so collected. He always got what he wanted, and yet he didn't seem . . . happy. There was something brewing beneath the surface, something stormy behind his eyes. It didn't make any sense.

The host barked out, "You're not perfect, sport. And let me save you the suspense: this girl you met? She's not perfect either."

I answered robotically, "*Good Will Hunting.*"

———

The next day on my lunch break, I sat with Chase in the atrium of the hockey arena. Outside his office. In plain sight on the well-worn industrial couches next to the windows across from the ticket booth.

It turned out he was able to find my email address. "What exactly is a compliance coach?" I asked to break the awkward silence.

Chase tapped his pen against the desk. "I'm a coach. With the responsibility of making sure the players stay compliant."

I gave him a look, and the corner of his mouth twitched.

"Hilarious."

Chase's eyes narrowed with a hint of amusement. "What exactly are you getting at, Maddie?"

"Madelyn."

His lips pinched, and he watched me a moment. Just as my cheeks started to heat, he said, "Did I do something to piss you off?"

Was he really asking that question? Either he was self-absorbed enough to be completely oblivious, or he was dumber than I thought.

"No. I think it was completely reasonable for my math professor to invite me to be on a compliance committee after a week of not hearing a word from you about my offer to tutor the players."

Chase's eyes widened a fraction.

I continued, "I guess that's why I'm asking this question. Because I thought a compliance coach would have jumped all over that. It's your job to help your players be successful. I offered help, and you did nothing about it."

"So you're mad I didn't ask you to be on the committee?" He looked at me like I was throwing a temper tantrum.

"No, Coach Wilson. I'm not mad. Just confused."

"So you want an explanation?"

"Only if you want to give it." So far, this conversation felt like trying to peel gum off the bottom of my shoe.

"I didn't invite you to be on the committee because, A, I wasn't aware we were inviting students, and, B." He held his breath, then exhaled in a rush. "I think the committee is bullshit."

I raised an eyebrow. "Again, you're the compliance coach—"

"My job is to get these kids playing." Chase leaned forward on the couch, resting his elbows on his knees and steepling his fingers together.

"Right. By helping get their grades up—"

"No. By badgering administration until they lower their expectations."

My brows pinched. "What?" *Was he messing with me again?*

"I get that to an idealist like you—"

"I'm not an idealist."

"Maddie—sorry, Madelyn—you offered to tutor students for free, out of the goodness of your heart."

I wet my lips. "Yes."

"And?"

"And what? Did you really not listen to a word I said when I came into your office?"

"I was a little distracted. It was unexpected—"

"Okay, whatever. I was trying to explain to you that I was looking for an opportunity to serve and lead here at Douglas because I'm applying for a scholarship."

He gave a slow nod, relaxing back in his seat. "Right. Okay. So you're not altruistic?"

"I'm not *not* altruistic. I still want to help them. Axel and Rory are my friends. And don't change the focus here. Are you saying that your job is to try and skirt the rules instead of supporting the players?"

He glanced around like I'd yelled it. "You won't find it in my job description. But that's what compliance coaches do."

"And you're okay with this?"

"It's my job."

"What, you had no other options?"

Something flickered behind Chase's eyes, and my stomach dropped. Maybe he *didn't* have any other options. I knew nothing about Chase's life. "I'm sorry. I didn't mean—"

"I had plenty of options, and I chose to take this one, where I get to be an asshole and fight with school administration. Is that what you want to hear?" He flipped open the cover on his notebook. "What can I write down that will make the committee feel as if we're supporting our student athletes? You should know since you're so good at brownnosing."

I ignored the immature dig. "Why don't you care about them getting their grades up?"

"It's not that I don't care."

"Then what? It seems like this committee could be a great thing."

"A great thing for who?"

I scoffed. "For your players. Their whole life isn't just going to be hockey. This education could be life-changing for them."

"Assuming they want it to be."

"Who doesn't want to have a good education?"

"See? Idealist." Chase rose from his chair and walked to the window, leaning back against the sill with his hands in his pockets. "When you were in high school, what was your plan?"

I folded my arms across my chest. "To get good grades and go to a good university."

Chase held out his hands. "And look, you've accomplished it." He paused a moment, and I started to fidget with the strap on my backpack. "Do you want to know what my plan was, Maddie?"

"Madelyn."

He ignored the correction. "My plan was to make it to the NHL." He gave a dramatic look to the right and then to the left. "Does it seem like that worked out for me?"

I pursed my lips. *Nope. It did not.* I didn't say it out loud.

Chase's expression sobered. "Some of us aren't built for school, and we've known that since kindergarten. Some of us pushed through because it was what we had to do in order to do the thing we really wanted, which was to play hockey.

"All of those guys out there—your friends—they don't play for a university team because that was their plan. All of them wanted to play Juniors. All of them wanted to make it to the AHL. All of them wanted to be drafted by a professional team by now.

"This is their backup plan. Madelyn. So if any of them are desperate to get a B or even an A in calculus, I'd be more than happy to support them in that. But I can tell you right now that none of them probably give a shit."

I drew a deep breath, working to slow my pulse. "Well,

maybe they *should* give a shit." I couldn't believe I was swearing in front of a faculty member, but he did it first.

Chase breathed a laugh. "Yeah. Well, my goal is to get them on the ice. Let them do the thing they love. After this, they're not going to have nearly as many opportunities."

My mind spun as a piece of the puzzle that was Chase Wilson clicked into place. He hadn't gotten everything he wanted. In high school, he'd sailed through. He'd been the hockey star, he'd gotten the girl, he'd moved out and become a legend—the guy who was going to make it big.

I cleared my throat. "But these guys are going to need to provide for themselves."

"You don't think they can provide for themselves with a C in calculus?" Chase asked dryly. "You know them better than I do. Do you see any of them going on to win a Nobel prize?"

My jaw tensed.

Chase pushed off the windowsill. "These restrictions are meant for administrators to feel good about themselves. They're not meant for the players." He dropped back onto the couch and picked up his notebook. "So. What would you like to recommend to appease Lamont and get Rory and Axel back on the ice?"

CHAPTER
Seven

IT WAS the kind of bright spring morning that made you *want* to believe in possibility. Crisp air, pale sun, wet pavement steaming like the earth itself was sighing in relief. I would've soaked it in had I not been trying to outpace Garrett. He'd stayed so late at Tash's capitalism study group that he'd crashed on our living room couch.

"Maddie! Wait up!"

I didn't. But since he was six-foot-four and had legs like a giraffe, he caught up anyway.

"Hey." He slid into step beside me, breath clouding slightly in the air, messenger bag slapping his hip. "Heading to class?"

I nodded. "Yep. Bright and early."

He grinned, catching his breath. "I have to cross campus to get home. Mind if I walk with you?"

I did, actually. But I lacked the social cruelty to say so outright. I looked him over. His clothes were rumpled, but he didn't look too dishevelled. "Did you get any sleep last night?"

"Oh, for sure. That couch is comfy."

"Your feet must've hung over the edge."

"No, it's the perfect length. The arm is at the perfect place for my knee crotch."

I snorted. "Please don't ever say that again."

His grin only widened. "Next time I could—"

"You're not sleeping in my room, Garrett." I was grinning now, too. I didn't know what to do with this. With him. On the one hand, I had to admit I was flattered. On the other, I'd never had a guy be so straight up.

Garrett was nice. Objectively attractive in that late-80s indie band kind of way—corduroy jacket, dark hair that curled around his ears. He had this lopey, happy-go-lucky energy that was contagious, but the idea of having a relationship with him? Kissing him?

That shut me down faster than Swackhammer's steakhouse with the oil bust. And it wasn't just Garrett. I'd dated. I'd tried. Colin, the guy I had my longest relationship with, had been good on paper. He was smart, sweet, into books. We had sex, and it was . . . fine. Perfectly acceptable. The kind of experience you'd circle "satisfactory" for on a customer service survey.

How pathetic was that? I convinced myself then that it was just the wrong match. We had no chemistry. After seeing Shar and Rob, I knew for a fact that was true. But now I wasn't so sure it was a Colin problem. Even after going out with a few other guys, I still didn't feel it—didn't know what it was supposed to feel like. Maybe I was the broken one. Maybe my brain was so amped up, I could never access that free, anti-analytical place.

Garrett shrugged. "It doesn't have to be anything serious. But you don't have a boyfriend, I don't have a girlfriend, and you're so beautiful, Maddie—"

I stopped mid-stride and turned to him. "Garrett. I really appreciate your determination and your kind words, but I'm focused on my education right now."

"Hey!"

I turned to see Crystal approaching. She was holding an extra coffee with my name on it. Garrett gave a small wave, his cheeks splotched with pink.

"Garrett. Any luck?" Crystal winked at him.

Garrett blew out a breath and shook his head. "I'd do whatever you want. Just sayin'." He adjusted his messenger bag, then shoved his hands in his pockets and kept walking.

Crystal handed me my coffee and waited before he was out of earshot before saying, "It could be fun, you know."

I rolled my eyes and walked toward the Coxeter building. While I understood the significance of the name, I don't think the university administrators recognized the low-hanging fruit they were offering students for innuendo. "I don't get how that would be fun."

Crystal laughed. "Because he'd be such a willing participant?"

"That's my literal nightmare. Me having to direct another human in . . . pleasure? Ugh." I shook out my hands. I didn't know my own body well enough to even know where to start.

Crystal took a sip of her coffee, holding it out and craning her neck so she didn't accidentally spill on her shirt while we strolled. "Just think about it as an experiment. You'd be collecting data."

"Nice try." I nudged her shoulder, not wanting to admit that her angle intrigued me. Not running an experiment with Garrett. That idea still made me queasy, but—

I blanched at the face that suddenly appeared in my head, then sucked in a breath at the instant tightening of my stomach. The rush of heat to my core.

"You okay?" Crystal gave me a sidelong glance.

I nodded too quickly. "Mmhmm. Just running a bit late." I gave her a hug and thanked her for the coffee, then split off at the path to head to class with Professor Kowalski. Damn it, why was Chase Wilson in my head? Especially while thinking about experimenting? Not considering it—that would be crazy—but the fact that it sounded even a little bit exciting . . . the fact that he was the one my brain attached to that feeling was very disconcerting.

Then again, it made perfect sense. The first time I ever felt that swoop in my stomach was when I walked down the hall and saw Chase leaning against the stairwell. What was it about him?

As I entered the classroom, I listed all the logical reasons why Chase would never—could never—be a good idea. He was older than me, my stepbrother, had a bad attitude, obviously didn't care about academics, and was a member of the Douglas University faculty. He was not someone to collect data with.

I rifled through the papers on Kowalski's desk and found my unit quiz. Ninety-eight percent.

"Be more careful with your proofs." Mr. Kowalski turned from the board, a piece of chalk in his hand. He nodded to the small red circle at the bottom of the fourth question. I shook my head. Rounding error.

The rest of the day passed in a blur of equations, symmetry groups, and note-scribbling until I landed in the library just after three with graphite smeared over the pad of my right hand and a low ache in my back. I collapsed into the chair at my favourite computer in the sunlit corner, logged in, and waited for my university email to populate.

When it did, I scrolled past the spam and ignored a message from my mom to click on the email with Lamont's name as the sender. *That was quick.* I tapped my fingers on the mouse as the screen went white, then began showing the message line by line.

Subject: Outlaws Academic Support Proposal – Additions

Madelyn and Coach Wilson,

Thank you for your thoughtful proposal. The committee was impressed with your outlined goals and strategies. We'd like to move forward with one small amendment.

In addition to the support plans you've submitted, we are asking that you offer twice-weekly optional study sessions for all participating athletes. It seems you have an excellent plan in place for those athletes currently on probation. We are willing to consider allowing them to participate in their practices and games as long as they are following this protocol.

However, we feel like more preventative care is needed. Our hope is that these study sessions will allow other players to catch up before they end up in crises. We'd like them to be co-supervised by both of you.

Madelyn, as discussed, I will be happy to keep a record of your efforts and volunteer hours as a part of this committee.

Please respond with your proposed schedule.

Best,

H.L.

I exhaled with relief. Well. That couldn't have gone better. Chase and I laid out a plan for moving Axel and Rory back into the green but didn't know if they'd go for it. Chase would be thrilled to have them back on the ice. But the twice-weekly study sessions? Based on his monologue the other day, I knew exactly what he'd say about them. It was posturing. Something the committee could hold up and show other faculty members as proof of their efforts.

As much as I hated to admit, he had a point. Would any of the Outlaws take us up on it? I chewed my lower lip. It definitely couldn't be at night. So many of them went out to Ranchman's after practice, and those who didn't went home and crashed. There was no way we'd convince them to give up that time to study. But before? That's when Rob was doing his extra work-outs, according to Shar, and weekends were out with games and tournaments.

Twice weekly. My mind poked and prodded the problem from different angles until something clicked.

Food. We needed to offer them food. Nothing big, but cook-ies? Brownies? We could hold the sessions on Tuesday and Wednesday to catch people regardless of their class stacks. Do one during lunch and one at three. Rob didn't usually start until four if I remembered correctly. We could hold them in the North Centre since it was close to the arena—The Douglas Dome. I still wasn't used to calling it that.

I leaned in and started typing.

Eight

THE NEXT DAY WAS TUESDAY, and while I hadn't met with Chase in person since our initial sit-down, he had responded with a "Sounds good" in reply to my suggestions for the study sessions. Very enthusiastic. Since I only had two words to over-analyze, I'd worked myself up into a slight frenzy after baking three dozen chocolate chip cookies the night before with Tash playing songs by a band called Bush in the background, complaining about how it was ridiculous that they were being told to change their name by some washed out band from the seventies. I smiled and nodded. Some of the songs were surprisingly good.

When I walked into the North Centre with my bowl of cookies, I walked fast. That way, I could blame rushing for my windedness and not the adrenaline coursing through my veins. It didn't matter if anyone showed up. Chase had emailed the team and promised he'd include the cookie details, but my confidence in his emailing ability was lower than a first-year's Calc 1 curve. I repeated the room number in my head and only walked the extra length of the hallway once before finding it. The door was closed, and there wasn't a window. I tried the handle and, when it turned, pushed the door open.

I scanned the room. Empty. But I was fifteen minutes early.

Setting my bowl of cookies on the desk, I pulled my hair back into a claw clip and dropped my bag next to the far end of one of the tables. This was a good setup. Four tables with chairs. There were no windows, which made it feel a bit claustrophobic, but there was a large chalkboard and projector. I looked up and found the cord for the pull-down screen. Not that I thought we'd be using it since I didn't have any transparencies, but if I needed to, I was sure I could borrow some from Kowalski.

I jumped as the door opened behind me.

"Oh. Hey. You're already here." Chase hesitated a second before entering. He wore jeans and a grey T-shirt today. *For the love, don't look at his forearms.*

"I arrived a couple of minutes ago." I moved behind the table. As if that would protect me from noticing . . . all of him.

Chase motioned at the bowl. "What's this?"

"See for yourself."

He strode forward and gingerly lifted the tinfoil. The smell of freshly baked cookies filled the room. His finger twitched, and I fought a smile. "You can have one."

He looked up at me through his lashes. "Are you sure? It looks like you don't have enough for the whole team to have two."

I gave him a look, and his eyes glittered. Then he did something that I can only describe as erotic. The word had never entered my vocabulary before, and I felt ridiculous even thinking it, but Chase didn't drop his eyes from mine as he reached into the bowl and picked up a cookie. The tinkling sound of the tinfoil shifting. The sight of his hand lifting something I'd made to his lips. The curve of his mouth as he took a bite. The soft sigh of pleasure as he chewed and swallowed.

Holy hell.

I blinked.

I wasn't thinking.

I dropped my eyes, breaking his hold on me, and seemed to

physically land back in the room. My fingers moved over the smooth laminate surface of the table. My toes wiggled in my shoes. Where had I gone? For those seconds, it was as if I hadn't existed. As if I'd been transported out of my thoughts, out of reality, and swept into some world where I only felt.

"That's a damn good cookie."

I swallowed hard. "That's . . . probably the nicest thing you've ever said to me." It was supposed to be a joke, but my voice was too breathy to pull it off.

Chase laughed. "Is it bad that I hope nobody shows up so I can have another one?"

"You hoped nobody showed up before you tried the cookies."

He did the little eye drop and exhale as he smiled. *Ugh.* I turned from the table and crouched, pretending to look for something in my backpack. What was happening to me? I was not one of those girls who melted in a guy's presence. Not that there was anything wrong with that—in fact, I wished I *was* one of those girls plenty of times when Colin touched me and tried to whisper something sexy while I lay there in the dark thinking about acute angles.

Now it felt like I'd been plucked up and dropped in the middle of a foreign country where I didn't speak the language. My palms started sweating. I glanced up at the sharp sound of a chair scraping across the floor.

Chase sat down, leaning back and lifting his arms behind his head. *Heaven help me.* "I think the guys will show up. But not until—" He peered at the clock. "About three forty-five."

I pulled out my notebook and pencil, completing my ruse. There was nothing I needed to write down. "Right before they hit the ice with Rob?" Chase nodded. When he said nothing else, I continued, "Because they'll want a cookie, but they don't give a shit about their classes."

"Exactly."

I pulled out the chair next to me and sat. "Well. You never know." Without looking up, I started doodling on the top corner of the page. Externally, I hoped I was pulling off being cool and collected because internally all I heard was: *Shit! Shit! Shit!*

Two hours. Chase and I had to be here for two hours together. If nobody showed up, what the hell were we going to do? I was already burning a hole in my underwear for reasons I didn't want to deconstruct at the moment, and I didn't have any homework to catch up on. No distractions. Nothing.

But—I clung to that 'but'—I had seen Rory and Axel that morning talking with Rob in the quad and told them about the study hours. The whole team had gotten the message about our new academic support plan, and Axel and Rory were already going to be working one-on-one with me and Chase to get things sorted with their professors and put in some extra credit. There was a chance that they'd show up before the end of our time, wasn't there?

The silence stretched, and the soft brush of my pencil against paper started to grate. I waited until I couldn't stand it anymore, then asked, "What were you doing before coming to Douglas?"

I was going for casual, but the truth was, I'd been curious about Chase's story from the second I saw him sitting on the Outlaws bench. What had happened to him? How had he ended up back here in Calgary, coaching, after his career had looked so promising?

He shrugged. "Couple years at U of C. Took classes. Worked construction. Did some coaching for a bantam team. Nothing special."

I stopped doodling and looked up. Chase stared at the door, his arms crossed over his chest. "And before that?" I couldn't help myself.

He glanced over but quickly looked away. "Uh, played for the Hitmen for a bit."

My eyes widened. "You were here in Calgary? After you left?"

He drew in a deep breath. "Played Juniors out in B.C. when I was seventeen. Got picked up by the Hitmen a year later.

Thought I was headed somewhere, but I wasn't drafted. Tried out for a couple of feeder teams, bounced around for a bit. By the time I was twenty, I knew it wasn't happening. Took a year off, worked, then started at U of C. Did part-time classes, part-time coaching. Finished my degree slowly—a bit here, a bit there. Not exactly a straight line."

I realized I was staring and dropped my gaze back to my paper, twisting the ring on my left hand. "And how did you end up at Douglas?"

Chase hesitated. "Got lucky, I guess."

That wasn't a real answer, but I didn't want to pry. I mean, I absolutely did want to pry, but by the tight set of his jaw, I decided it wasn't socially prudent.

"What about you?" He shifted in the chair, and the plastic creaked.

"Definitely a straight line."

He nodded once. "No surprises there."

"What do you mean by that?" I rested my arms over my notebook. Chase finally met my eyes, but he didn't answer. "Are you saying I'm boring?"

The corner of his mouth lifted. "I would never criticize an honest pursuit of academics."

My eyes narrowed. "How can you even talk? You already got your degree."

"I'm not knocking school."

"Just people who *prioritize* it?" I tucked my curls behind my ear. "You did what you loved, and I did what I loved. How is one better than the other?"

"Well, you didn't fail at yours yet, so I'd say you're winning."

I opened my mouth, then shut it. Our two trajectories appeared in my head like a line graph. Both of us heading straight up toward our goals and then . . . "I'm sorry hockey didn't—"

"Yo! This the right room?" The door swung open with a bang, and I jumped. Axel appeared first, a family-sized bag of All-

Dressed Old Dutch chips in one hand. Rory followed, slinging his backpack onto the table.

"Are these the cookies?" Rory peeled back the tinfoil and grabbed two. Chase's jaw ticked.

I breathed a sigh of relief. It wasn't even close to three forty-five. "You guys came."

Axel strode toward me, his arms outstretched. "Wouldn't miss it, Maddie girl." I stood, and he gave me a huge bear hug.

Chase pushed his chair back and stretched out his legs. He looked like he was about to take a nap. "I thought you boys already had plans to meet with your professors this week."

"Can't get too early a jump on it, eh?" Rory dropped into the chair next to me.

I gave Chase a smug look. "No, you can't." I sat as both of them pulled out their books. Applied math for Rory and Calc for Axel, if I was remembering correctly. He was an engineering major. I couldn't remember if Rory had declared or not.

"Proportional reasoning and function notation." Rory said the words like he was announcing someone had died.

Axel opened his text. "Derivatives. You're welcome."

I grinned. Now this was a language I understood. I started with Rory, walking him through slope and rate of change, only to be met with blinking confusion.

Axel didn't do much better.

"So you take the function," I explained, pointing at the equation, "and then you derive it. You take the exponent, multiply it by the coefficient—"

I stopped when I noticed his blank stare. "You know what. Let's try something different." I stood and walked to the chalkboard. Thankfully, there was one half piece of chalk lying in the metal gutter.

I lifted it and drew a line. "Okay. Picture this. You're skating full speed toward the net, but the puck's getting away from you. What's changing?"

Axel stared at the board. I waited until he finally said. "Speed?"

"Exactly. But you're not just looking at how fast you're going. You're watching how your speed is changing in relation to the puck. That's a derivative. It's rate of change."

Axel's face lit up. "Ohhh. Like acceleration."

"Exactly."

I pivoted to Rory, scrambling for an analogy that would work for him. We were looking for performance over time which kind of translated perfectly with hockey. I just had to choose a metric. "Okay, for function notation. Let's say your shot percentage is a function of ice time." I turned to the board and scribbled: $f(x) =$ shot % based on x minutes on the ice. "So $f(x)$ is how well you shoot depending on how long you're on the ice. If we plug in thirty minutes of game time—$f(30)$—what do we get?"

"A broken stick and ten minutes in the penalty box?" Axel leaned back in his chair like he was waiting for applause.

Rory elbowed him with a crooked grin. "Try a goal or two."

I laughed. "Perfect. Because what we're looking for isn't only the number of shots. We're looking for the output of a relationship—something measurable that changes as your input does."

Rory's brow furrowed, but the wheels in my head were spinning at full speed. "No, this is amazing. Think of it like this. If we want to know how effective you are in a game, we're not just looking at your total shots. We're looking at what you do *per minute* of ice time. We want to know, 'If I put Rory on the ice for ten more minutes, what's the expected outcome?' That's your function. $f(x)$ tells him what to expect at x minutes."

Rory blinked. "So like . . . $f(10)$ might be one goal, but $f(30)$ might be four?"

"Pfft. Try two." Axel teased.

"Yes!" I grinned. "Exactly that." I gave a nod to Axel. "And if your percentage starts to drop the longer you're out there, the function can show that, too. I would say coaches probably use this kind of thinking all the time. How else would they decide to rotate lines?"

He squinted at the equation again, then nodded, slowly. "So it's kind of like my whole performance, graphed."

I stared at what I'd written on the board. Holy shit. That's exactly what this was. "Yeah. It tells you what output you get at a certain input. Like a vending machine. You press A6, you get a Coffee Crisp. You press A7, you get a sad granola bar."

Axel exhaled. "Tragic."

Rory turned the example over in his head, then reached for his pencil and started copying down the formula. "That makes way more sense. When I read it in the book, it made no sense."

I couldn't help smiling. "Math is code for patterns. You already know the patterns. You're just not used to seeing them written down."

Rory looked up. "Do coaches use this?"

I turned my head to find Chase watching me. "I don't know. Do they?"

Rory and Axel turned, waiting for an answer.

Chase cocked his head to the side. "It's a little more intuitive."

Intuitive? There was nothing intuitive about this. Our brains paid attention to sensory data inconsistently and magnified the importance of some things more than others. The only way to know how these guys performed on the ice was by looking at the numbers.

"You know our functions?" Axel waggled an eyebrow.

There was that eye drop. The gentle exhale. The ache was back in my middle. "Nope. I'm only the compliance coach."

Only. Another piece of the puzzle. Was Chase happy with this job? Or did he want more?

"So what next?" Rory asked.

I set the chalk back in its silver bed. "Now you do problem sets." Rory balked. "Don't worry, I'll help you."

Axel raised his hand. "And then cookies?"

Chase grunted. "You've already inhaled half the bowl."

Rory grinned. "Yeah, but now we're earning them."

The rest of the session sped past. I helped both of them with their problem sets, thrilled that they actually understood. By the end, they were getting most of their answers right without any input from me.

"When we talk to your professors tomorrow, you're going to show them this." I slipped my notebook into my bag.

Rory looked hesitant. "What if I don't remember any of this tomorrow?"

"No problem. We'll go through more questions. Math is about repetition. Patterns of thinking change with practice. And the good news is, with your other classes, it's mostly memorization. I have tricks for that, too."

Axel jumped up and took a cookie from the bowl. "Can I take these to practice?"

I started to shake my head, then thought better of it. "Actually, yes. But tell the boys they won't get anything else unless they show up to studying sessions."

Chase stood and sauntered to the bowl. I gave him a look as he reached in and took two cookies. "What? I showed up to the studying session."

I fought a grin as my chest warmed. The fact that he loved my cookies shouldn't have made me feel more proud than I did when I got that quiz back from Kowalski. But it did.

Axel and Rory packed up, and Axel grabbed the bowl. "I promise you'll get this back."

"I better."

Rory swooped back and gave me a hug. "Maddie girl. You're the best."

I blushed at the flattery as they left, then scooped up my own bag and slid the straps over my shoulders.

Chase sighed. "Go ahead. Say it."

I glanced up. "Say what?"

"That I was wrong."

I couldn't tamp down the smile that time. "You were only partially wrong. The other guys didn't show up. You called that."

"I didn't know you were such good friends with them."

"With Axel and Rory?"

He nodded, brushing cookie crumbs from his lip.

"They're good guys. And I think they care more than you give them credit for." I adjusted my bag on my back. "Maybe they just need one person to believe they can be more than what they are."

Chase's jaw worked. I gave him a nod, then turned to the door. When I was almost over the threshold, he said, "Will you walk me through those functions? For the team?"

I turned back. "I thought it was intuitive."

Chase shrugged. "I thought you were a teacher's pet."

"Teachers. Not coaches. There's a difference."

His lips twitched. "Smart ass." I mimed a curtsy, and he laughed. "I haven't seen anyone run numbers like that. It could be helpful. Especially with Canada West coming up."

The Canada West University Hockey Championship. Last year, the Outlaws had just missed qualifying for the CIAU University Cup—the national championship held each spring. "I could do that."

Chase drew in a breath. "Are you—do you have plans now?"

I wet my lips, my brain short-circuiting. Did I have plans? I couldn't think past Chase standing with his hands in his pockets in front of me. "No. I don't have plans. But—"

"But what?"

My stomach grumbled. "I will need to eat at some point." Unlike him, I hadn't downed four cookies in the last hour.

Chase's mouth quirked. "I can take care of that."

CHAPTER
Nine

WE EXITED the North Centre under a sky smeared with bright spring colours. The days were getting longer, and I could almost smell the tailgate barbecues. Students still did them in the winter, but they were so much better when I wasn't worried about smearing my winter coat with ketchup.

I was suddenly hyperaware of everything I did. How I walked, how I held my bag. Chase was just close enough that I could smell whatever soap he used—something clean and masculine. Had I even noticed what Garrett smelled like?

Chase didn't say much until we turned down the path that curved toward the Dome. A little café slash corner store was tucked beside the arena, squeezed between the players' entrance and the main doors.

He pointed. "Does that work?"

"For what?"

He slowed. "For dinner."

I hesitated. "I guess—"

"I'll get it, I just wondered—"

"You don't have to get it." I didn't want him to think my comment was a plea for help.

Chase stopped on the sidewalk. "You're doing me—the team

—a favour. I'm not going to make you pay for your food when you were probably heading home."

I was heading home. But it wasn't like I had great options there at the moment. I was probably going to make myself a bowl of canned soup.

"C'mon." He started down the path, and I followed.

"Chase—"

"Coach Wilson." He gave me a sidelong glance.

I exhaled. "Okay, I'm sorry I was being pissy about my name."

Chase laughed. "You were being pissy."

"You didn't email me."

"I already explained—"

"Yeah, I know. You think this whole thing is bullshit. Your words, not mine."

He slowed as we approached the entrance then reached out and held the door for me. I stared at it then at him with his arm outstretched. "This is weird."

"Yeah."

"If we acknowledge it, will it be less weird?"

Chase's lips twitched. "Doubtful."

"That's what I thought." I walked through the door. Inside, the café was warm and smelled like fresh bread. There were three small tables along the window, a short counter for ordering, and a few aisles with bags of candy, snacks, and emergency essentials. One table was occupied by a couple of tired-looking students in Douglas hoodies, their trays piled high with fries. The board above the counter offered daily specials in wonky chalk handwriting: tomato soup, grilled ham and cheese, and something called a Dome Power Bowl.

Chase ordered the fried chicken sandwich. I went for the Caesar salad with grilled chicken, not because I wanted to look like I was eating healthy, but because I hadn't ingested vegetables since Saturday. And I doubted onion rings even counted.

He handed the cashier a couple of bills, and we stood off to the side to wait.

"You said you coached before?"

Chase nodded. "With a couple of different teams, but not at the university level."

"Wasn't part of the plan?"

He fingered a package of gummy worms. "Not initially."

I couldn't handle these two-word answers, and while he'd given me a few details of his life, it hadn't scratched the itch in the least. I wanted more. And maybe if we actually talked about the interim between now and when we'd seen each other last, some of this tension I felt would disappear. Maybe it was the mystery of it that was making my body go haywire.

"What happened? After you left?"

Chase turned and started to answer, then stopped himself. "How long did he stay?"

I knew instantly who he was talking about. His dad. I wrapped my arms around myself involuntarily. "About three months." It might've been less than that, but I remembered the day my mom finally changed the locks. I'd just gotten back from Calaway Park with my friend Kate, and there was a pile of his things on the front porch.

"I felt bad about that." Chase looked up at the menu board, his jaw tight. "Leaving you both with him."

My ribs seemed to cinch around my lungs. He felt bad? I didn't think he'd given us a second thought. "You were barely ever there."

He scrubbed his hand over the stubble on his jaw. "Yeah."

Another little puzzle piece. Was it possible that Chase wasn't out at all hours of the night because he was cool and popular? Was it because . . . he didn't want to be home?

My whole worldview tipped on its axis. I rewound the tape and searched for all the times he was at the house. It was usually in the afternoon, right after school or in the morning on the weekends. What seventeen-year-old was up at eight thirty in the morning on a Saturday? I couldn't help it. I still wasn't able to sleep in, even after staying up until two in the morning. Naps had become my friend since coming to Douglas.

Chase exhaled. "I wasn't stupid enough to think I'd make it straight to the NHL, but hockey was my best option to get out."

I chewed on that for a moment. "It's not stupid to go for something big. And you were so good."

"'Were' being the operative word there."

Tension radiated off of him. I lowered my voice. "Injury?"

He shook his head. "Nope. Just not good enough."

The woman at the counter held up his sandwich and my salad, and Chase stalked forward to take them. He smiled and thanked her, and I followed him to the door.

We walked through the main entrance and down the hall. Chase unlocked the door to the hockey offices with a grunt and a shoulder nudge. The door stuck a little in the frame, and there was no receptionist to greet us this time. What time was it? "Do you need to be at practice?"

Chase glanced at the clock above the door. Four fifteen. "It's fine if I'm a bit late, but we still have forty-five minutes."

We passed the front desk and entered one of the small offices in the short hall. He flicked on the light even though there was plenty of sunlight coming in from the full window in the door. This was a welcome change from the study room.

A corkboard hung on the wall crowded with player sched-ules and tournament flyers, and a hockey stick leaned against the filing cabinet like it might be called into action at any moment. Was it his?

Chase dropped his sandwich onto the desk and rifled through a drawer. I took the rolling chair in front of the desk and opened the lid on my salad. Normally I'd wait until whoever I was with started eating, but my stomach lining was beginning to digest itself. I took a bite, and the crisp lettuce and tangy dressing sent a flavour burst through my mouth.

"Good?"

I glanced up. Chase held a thick folder in one hand. "Mmh-mm," I mumbled while chewing.

His mouth quirked as he pushed the folder toward me on the desk. "Shot counts, time on ice, zone entries. Last six games."

I brushed my hand on my jeans and flipped over the cover, taking in the highlighter markings and cramped handwriting. He was thorough, I'd give him that. There wasn't a single missed entry.

I swallowed and scanned the data. It was messy, but the patterns started to jump out fast. "Do you have baseline numbers?"

He grabbed a second folder. "First semester. November and December."

I nodded, flipping pages, salad temporarily forgotten. "You've got Axel starting in the offensive zone way more than anyone else." I tapped the page. "But you're not adjusting for that. It makes his possession look way better than it is."

He blinked. "Should I be?"

"Only if you want accurate data."

I scribbled a quick adjustment on the edge of the sheet, showing how weighting by zone starts gave a clearer picture of who was driving play.

Chase sat and unwrapped his sandwich. "I didn't know I could feel so useless in such a short amount of time."

"Hm. Not useless." I gestured to my salad.

He chuckled. I was already halfway back inside the numbers. I frowned at one of the sheets and tapped the top corner. "Wait—what's this column? Plus-minus?"

Chase leaned over, a piece of lettuce stuck to his thumb. "Yeah. It's the goal differential stat—shows how many goals were scored for or against while a player was on the ice. Doesn't include power plays or penalty kills, just even strength."

I blinked. "So . . . if your team scores while you're out there, you get a plus. If they get scored on, you get a minus?"

"Exactly. People say it's flawed, but it gives a snapshot. Tells you if a player's generally on the ice when good or bad things happen."

I nodded, letting that click into place. "So you could play solid defense and set up beautiful plays, but if your goalie lets in a soft one, you get dinged?"

"Pretty much. But over a season, it starts to show patterns. Scouts pay attention to it, especially when they want to know who's reliable in close games."

I glanced back down at the page. "Huh. Then Bear's getting screwed."

"What?"

I shifted the paper so he could see. "He's got a rough plus-minus, but look at who he's out with and when. He's starting nearly every shift in the defensive zone. No support, no momentum. Of course his numbers are trash."

Chase blinked. Bear's plus-minus was deep in the red, but it didn't take long to see why—he was constantly deployed in the worst possible scenarios. Late shifts, heavy forecheck from the other team, and line changes that left him stranded. He wasn't sloppy. He was set up to fail. With a better rotation, he could hold the blue line better than half the roster.

"Damn." Chase's brows pinched.

I picked up on other patterns. Nick and Bear had solid synergy, but only when paired together. Their shot suppression went up dramatically when they were on the ice at the same time. Split them up and their efficiency tanked. I circled it and made a note: keep them as a unit.

And then there was Rob. His power play stats were impressive, as were his shots and goals. No surprise there.

I flipped to Logan's sheet and pursed my lips. I didn't hate the guy since he'd put on his big boy pants and apologized to Shar, but he still wasn't my favourite person. But numbers didn't take into account personal feelings.

"Impressive, right?"

I nodded. "No wonder he was scouted." I exhaled and leaned

back in my chair, fingers smudged, my head somehow clearer than it had been all week.

Chase swallowed his bite of sandwich. I hadn't even realized he was eating. "So who sucks at the penalty kill?"

"Tim, but I didn't need to look at the stats to tell you that."

Lowered eyes, a small puff of air, and that smile. Chase wadded up the parchment paper and threw it in the trash. "I should've emailed you. About the tutoring."

"This was all it took to convince you?" I took another forkful of salad.

He picked up a pen from his desk and fiddled with it. "Maybe I was caught up in my own shit. I wasn't remembering."

My breathing slowed. "Remembering what?"

He shrugged. "How good you are at this. The math, but more so the teaching."

I swallowed. "I really don't understand how you could forget. You aced your Math 20 midterm because of me."

Chase didn't speak. Just watched me.

Right there. *It was moments like this.*

He'd always been throwing curveballs, never responding as I expected him to. That's what gave him such an air of mystery in high school. I could never tell exactly what he was thinking. That damn puzzle I couldn't solve.

His gaze made me self-conscious enough that I reached for the highlighter sitting in a wooden pen holder on the desk. In the process I knocked it over, sending his writing utensils sprawling.

"I'm so sorry, I—"

"It's fine. Here." Chase started scooping up the pens and pencils, while I again went for the highlighter, and somehow, my hand was suddenly trapped between his.

We both froze. My fingertips logged every modicum of sensory input available to them. His palm was warm. Rougher than mine. His fingers extended past my wrist—I hadn't realized his hands were so large.

And my brain? Misfiring. Because I enjoyed this feeling, and it felt as if I'd been waiting for it. Thirsting to feel him. Like I'd been biding my time since . . . well, since I was fourteen. Since I'd seen his hand tapping a rhythm on my kitchen counter.

Now here I was. Taking full stock of the heat flashing over my skin, the tingling at my fingertips, the shortness of breath. Here I was *collecting data.*

I yanked my hand back, sending the highlighter flipping into my lap. "I was—so you're bleeding possession minutes on your third line." I pulled the sheet toward me and clicked the cap off the pen. "Swap Axel in when you're up a goal. He can eat the zone time and buy you breathing room."

Chase dropped the pens back in the wooden box. "Noted."

CHAPTER
Ten

THE BLEACHERS of the Douglas Dome were already buzzing when I squeezed between Shar and Crystal, nearly dropping my smoothie in the process. It wasn't warm enough to justify an iced drink under normal circumstances, but once the temperature hit ten degrees Celsius in Alberta after a long winter, it was basically shorts weather.

The smell of popcorn, rubber, and that industrial cleaner they used on the concrete floors hit me like it always did—familiar and comforting, but tonight? It also heightened my nerves. Tuesday evening, I'd handed the file back to Chase, and I had no idea what he was going to do with it. He wasn't sure if Coach Blakely would even consider letting him mess with the shifts, but I crossed my fingers. The data didn't lie.

And tonight, the Outlaws were playing Red Deer Central College's team, the Ravens. When we played them on their home ice earlier in the season, they beat us in a shootout.

I found Chase pacing behind the bench, his shirt sleeves rolled up. I bit my lip.

"I've never liked this team," Crystal muttered, eyeing the Red Deer bench. Their jerseys were deep red with silver piping, and their goalie looked like he could bench-press a Zamboni.

Shar nudged me. "You look like you're about to puke."

I'd filled the girls in on my meeting with Chase, but as soon as their eyes started to glaze over, I'd skipped ahead to the accidental finger brush, and we'd spent the rest of the conversation on my near panic attack and subsequent highlighter flip.

"I get it, you know. The patterns. Music is math, too." Sharla threw an arm over my shoulders and squeezed. "It's like you're the conductor. You give the best instruction you can and hope everyone else follows." Her brows pinched. "Huh. I never thought about how stressful that is."

"Only if you care about the finished product." Crystal leaned over and took a swig of my smoothie.

I tried to keep my voice casual, but my fingers were clamped so tightly around the styrofoam cup it creaked. "Chase was talking about how this is one of the last opportunities these guys will get to play competitive hockey. That's sad, isn't it?"

Shar cocked her head to the side. "It is, yeah. But it's kind of the same for us. When will I get to play in an orchestra like this again?"

I considered that. "You could audition, couldn't you?"

"I mean, that's the goal, but if I don't make it, I'm in the same boat as the players. Stuck in community groups—not that that's a bad thing, but it's not as high level."

Crystal nodded. "At least you'll never age out."

Shar blew out a breath. "That's true. And my arm hopefully won't give out as fast from bowing as Rob's knees will from sprinting on the ice."

The first puck drop had barely hit the ice before I saw it. The third line was starting the shift. Not Rob's line. Not Axel's. I clapped a hand over my mouth. Chase had convinced Blakely to roll a lower-energy line first to offset the expected first-period push, that was the only explanation.

"Isn't that new?" Shar frowned.

"Yup," I murmured. "Saving Axel for when the pace drops a

hair. Letting the other team burn themselves out against our grinders."

Crystal blinked at me. "I'm just going to cheer and scream at the refs instead of trying to make sense of that, cool?"

I laughed. When I looked up, Chase stood still at the back of the box, his eyes locked on mine. My face lit up, and I pointed at the ice using my arms as sideways exclamation points. Even from here, his head dip was visible as a smile split his face. He glanced back up and gave a cheeky shrug.

Two minutes in, the puck was deep in the Ravens' zone. Bear scooped it behind their net, passed back to Rob at the point, and *bam*.

Goal.

"One-nothing!" Crystal shrieked, jumping to her feet.

But I barely noticed the scoreboard change. All I saw was the zone entry timing. Chase had timed the line shift perfectly.

Midway through the first period, Red Deer tried to press back, but every time they attempted a breakout, Nick and Rory collapsed the neutral zone like they'd rehearsed it. I could feel my heartbeat in my fingertips.

The second period saw Bear and Rory out longer than usual, and at first, I thought it was a mistake. Then I noticed the staggered pairing. Rory's stats might not sparkle, but with Bear covering defensively, he had more freedom to play instinctively.

By the time Axel roofed a backhander on a power play in the second period, after one of their forwards drew a penalty crashing the net, we were up three-nothing.

Shar leaned over and whispered, "Your brain is terrifying."

I grinned. "Math, suckers!"

Red Deer finally scored halfway through the third. Their centre got loose after a turnover and popped it glove-side. The Ravens' bench roared. But it was too little, too late.

Chase didn't flinch. Blakely called for the third line again to slow the tempo. Then Axel and Rob came out and executed the shift Chase had drawn up Tuesday.

Another goal.

Four-one.

When Axel deked past two defenders in the final minute and tapped in a rebound, the whole place exploded.

Five-one. *Holy shit.*

The final buzzer sounded, and students pressed toward the glass, pounding their hands and shouting.

"That was—I don't even know, that's the best I've ever seen them play!" Crystal stood with both hands clawed in her hair, staring at our friends on the ice.

I didn't yell. I didn't move.

My eyes were laser-focused on Chase behind the bench. He was talking with Blakely as the guys celebrated, and then, as Rob led the team back through the gate to exit the rink, Chase turned.

He scanned the ice, the scoreboard, then dragged his eyes to our section. When he found me, he straightened, then pointed. When he was sure he had my attention, he moved his hand to his shoulder and brushed, like he was flicking off a piece of lint.

I laughed out loud.

"What?" Crystal followed my eye line and planted her hands on her hips. "Are you flirting from across the whole damn arena?"

"No!" I groaned, turning and grabbing her arm, pulling her toward the stairs. Shar was already halfway down the row.

"Rob's meeting us at Ranchman's!" She called back over her shoulder.

The wind had kicked up during the game, but nobody seemed to care. The parking lot buzzed like a live wire— students who hadn't cared about hockey two weeks ago were practically doing cartwheels over the Outlaws' 5–1 blowout. We were surrounded by endless honking and bodies hanging out of side door windows.

Crystal clutched my arm. "You might be a witch."

I laughed, giddy and flushed with adrenaline. "Don't tell anyone. They'll burn me at the stake."

We didn't have to walk far to reach my Rabbit. Thanks to my heightened anxiety levels, I'd arrived early to the game. I unlocked the driver's side door with a satisfying *ka-chunk*, reached around and unlocked the other doors, and we piled in.

"I can't believe Blakely actually listened." Shar turned up the volume on the radio.

"I don't know much about him." I reversed, claiming a spot in the winding line of cars waiting to exit the lot.

"He doesn't strike me as a pushover." Crystal leaned forward between the two seats.

"Well, apparently he's willing to listen to reason."

"And it *worked*. So, what is Chase now? Assistant coach?"

I scoffed. "I doubt he even wants that." After the words left my lips, I questioned them. What did Chase want? He'd all but admitted he didn't have a lot of options when it came to coaching. Was that why he asked me to help him? Was he looking for a way to position himself into a better coaching position?

"I saw that look he gave you. It wasn't just a 'thanks for helping me.' If you know what I mean." Crystal winked at me in the rearview mirror.

"Dude, tell him to shave that mustache and I'd be all in on wanting him for you."

I snorted. "Why, thank you for—"

The car in front of me screeched to a halt, and I slammed on the brakes, stopping centimetres from the guy's bumper. I sucked in a breath, white-knuckling the wheel. Then all of us burst out laughing.

It took more than fifteen minutes to get to Ranchman's, but it didn't kill our buzz. The bar was somehow already half-full by the time we arrived, the scent of cologne, burgers, and fries so thick, it steamed up the windows.

Crystal grabbed my arm and hauled me through the crowd. We always made a beeline for the reserved tables at the back. They were technically set aside for the players, but since Shar was with Rob, we counted.

Two pitchers of beer and a basket of peanuts were already waiting for us.

"Ugh. This place is the best." Crystal grabbed a stool and settled in.

The door swung again, and in streamed the Outlaws with their damp hair and wide grins. Rob, Bear, Axel, and Rory were instantly mobbed. It took them a full ten minutes to reach the back. Rob scooped Shar into his arms and planted a kiss on her lips. She melted into him, her fingers lifting into his hair.

I wanted that. But for the first time, I wasn't looking at Rob or whatever guy my friends were dating. I was looking at them. At Shar. Here, in the middle of all the chaos, she let herself go. If I wanted what she and Rob had, I needed to be like that. I had no idea where to start.

Rob pulled back and kissed her temple.

"Good game." Shar ruffled his hair.

Axel plopped down next to Crystal and snagged a handful of peanuts. "You three are officially good luck. You're not allowed to skip any more games." He turned to me. "And you. You're now required to meet with Coach Wilson before every game, eh?"

I laughed and took the beer Rory poured for me. "I can do that."

"Cheers." Rory held up his glass, and the others hustled to fill theirs and clink.

We ordered wings, nachos, and eventually switched to drinking Diet Cokes and lemon water. Everyone was laughing. Teasing. Celebrating. Axel started in on telling us about his aunt or great aunt or someone he was related to who was letting us stay in their house for the weekend after Canada West.

As exciting as that was, I couldn't stop scanning the door. It was twenty minutes later, and I was halfway through a bite of buffalo chicken, when the door swung open and Chase walked in.

My chest lifted—immediate and involuntary—only to slam down like a brick two seconds later. Because sweeping in behind him, her arm linked with his, was Melody Sanchez.

CHAPTER
Eleven

"WHAT'S WRONG, MADDIE?" Crystal reached over me to grab a wing.

"Oh. Nothing." I scooped my curls back from my face and stared intently at the bowl of ranch dressing.

"Uh-huh." Crystal dipped her wing, then leaned in. "It has nothing to do with the fact that Coach Wilson just walked in. With a hot brunette wearing a motorcycle jacket."

I didn't even pretend this time. Instead, I curled into her and hissed, "It's the girl he used to date in high school."

Crystal's eyes widened as she used both hands to eat her wing in the style of old cartoon characters eating corn on the cob. When she was finished, she set down the picked-clean bone and wiped her fingers with a napkin. "Shut up. You know her?"

I nodded, keeping my voice low so we wouldn't attract the attention of the rest of the team. "I hated her for all of grade nine."

Crystal made a cradle with her hands and dropped her chin into it. "Tell me more."

"She didn't deserve my hatred. It's just that I was a little—"

"Obsessed with Chase? Yes. I'm aware."

I groaned and curled into myself. "I don't know. I had this

weird secret world I was living in. The one where Chase paid attention to me and noticed me, but it only existed outside of school when we were at home doing math at the island, which really only happened once or twice a week. But it felt like those moments were bigger than everything else combined. And even if he didn't so much as look at me in the hallway at school, it didn't matter. It felt like it was our secret code, like we had something that nobody else knew about. And then he left, and I realized there was *no secret world*. It was just me. Alone. Fantasizing about a nonexistent relationship with Chase Wilson."

I froze and glanced around the table. I said that louder than intended, but it didn't seem like anybody noticed.

Crystal turned my face back to hers. "He recognized you here, didn't he?"

I nodded with a slow exhale. "He knew who I was. Big whoop." But there was that moment in his office when our hands touched. That had happened before. One time in the kitchen when I'd reached for my glass of water to fill it up, he took it from me.

"You're helping me with my homework, Maddie. At least let me get you some water."

That one line made my whole week.

A pit opened up in my stomach. *Another puzzle piece?*

Chase hadn't asked me to his office because he wanted to spend time with me. He asked me there because he needed something from me. That was exactly why he'd spent time with me in high school, too, wasn't it? He wanted help with math?

No, back then he'd never explicitly asked me to do it, but I'd been more than a willing participant. On Tuesday, he asked for my help, and I, like an idiot, dropped everything and followed him like a lost puppy to his office.

And now here we were again. Him celebrating the B+ on his math test and showing up with Melody Sanchez on his arm.

I squeezed Crystal's hand. "I think I'm going to head home. Can you get a ride with Rob and Shar?" Crystal frowned, but I didn't give her a chance to convince me to stay. I reached over and squeezed Sharla's shoulder. "Hey. Can Crystal go home with you guys? I need to run."

She nodded and disentangled herself from Rob to give me a hug. "Have a good night, Maddie."

"Yeah. You too."

"Maddie!" Crystal called out, but I was already on my way to the door.

I almost made it. I pushed through the excited fans and kept my head low. But as I reached for the door handle, a hand gripped my wrist, tugging me back. A jolt shot through my arm, and I sucked in a breath as I turned.

Chase stood in front of me with a huge grin on his face. He glanced down at where he touched me and dropped my arm, then cleared his throat. "You weren't even going to say hello?"

My eyes flitted to Melody, who scooted in to stand beside him, threading her arm through his. I forced a smile. "You seemed occupied."

Chase's mouth quirked. "You remember Melody?"

I did indeed. I remembered her more than he did, if our post-washroom conversation was to be believed. "I doubt she remembers me."

She laughed, throwing out a hand. "Of course I do! You're Chase's little sister."

Everything inside me crumbled. "Hm. Yeah, we're not—"

"Were you at the game tonight?" She clung tighter to Chase's arm. "I heard it was wild."

I nodded, glancing briefly at Chase before avoiding his gaze like it was the last Timbit on a road trip. "It was . . . pretty incredible. You weren't there?"

She sighed. "Nope. Couldn't make it, but Chase met me after."

After. It took me two point five seconds to do that math. The game ended around eight thirty, and it was now ten forty-two.

The numbers didn't lie.

I forced a smile. "So nice to see you again. I hope you have a great night." I spun on my heel and pushed through the door.

———

I woke up with a pounding head and a numb left arm. Blinking, I rolled and cringed at the sensation of prickling needles under my skin as the blood re-entered my limb. *What the hell was that sound?*

A shrill ringing sounded from the other room, and I finally connected that it was the telephone. I checked my alarm clock to see it was seven fifty-five in the morning, then groaned into my pillow before rolling out of bed in nothing but an oversized tee and my boy-shorts underwear.

Tash was up later than I was the night before, and she was going to kill me if that phone call was for me. If it was for her? I'd smother her with a pillow.

"I'm coming, I'm coming," I muttered, stumbling barefoot over a laundry pile and stubbing my toe on the baseboard as I entered the kitchen.

I picked up the receiver and croaked, "Hello?"

"Oh good, you're alive."

I pulled to release the cord so I could sit at the table, then immediately regretted it. The chair was freezing on my half-bare butt cheeks. "Hi, Mom."

She huffed like she'd been holding her breath. "You haven't called all week. I was about to send a Mountie to your apartment."

"Sorry." I yawned. "I've been so busy."

"Maddie. I'm your mother. I've known you since before you could pronounce 'hypotenuse.' A five-minute call won't collapse your GPA."

That made me grin. She was right, as usual. "I was asked to be on a committee. To help with student athletes."

"What? When?"

"It's been the past two weeks. I was looking for something I could do to—"

"Make your application more impressive. For the Rhodes?"

I don't know why it warmed my heart that she remembered. Of course she did. "Exactly. And the team has been struggling since Logan left."

"Well, I heard about their big win last night. They mentioned it on the radio this morning—5-1, wasn't it?"

"Yeah."

"Against Red Deer?"

"Yup. Ravens." For a brief moment, I thought about telling her everything. The drama with Chase, the adjustments I helped make to their game strategy. But this morning, it all suddenly felt empty. It was stupid that I felt so gutted by nothing.

Chase probably hadn't done any of this on purpose. He probably had no clue I felt the way I did because I barely knew what I felt. I needed to stop letting my emotions cloud my purpose. I'd done what I intended to. I helped my friends. I was participating in a worthy cause on campus. None of the rest of it mattered.

"I saw Cliff in Safeway yesterday." Mom's voice was soft, almost apologetic.

I blinked. "What?" It took me a moment to compute what she was saying. "Cliff as in Cliff Wilson?" That was Chase's dad, and the mention of him in the midst of thinking about Chase was disorienting.

"We talked. I know I should've walked the other direction, but . . . I don't know. He seemed sad."

"Mom—"

"I know, I know, but it wasn't all bad. He said Chase is coaching now. Something about a compliance job?"

Blood rushed in my ears. "Oh?"

"Yeah, I guess Cliff had some connection with a University or something and was able to get him the job."

My heart sped, and I suddenly felt dizzy.

"I think he's really struggled since high school," Mom continued. "He and Cliff never got along—no surprise there—but everything with his mom—"

"What about his mom?"

"Oh . . . I . . . well, I'm not sure if it's common knowledge, but his mom is in prison."

It felt like a fist punched through my sternum. "In prison? For what?"

Mom sighed. "It was a DUI. Really sad, actually. She ended up killing a pedestrian. I think she got seven years so—actually, she might be getting out soon."

My stomach twisted. I pushed up from the chair, bracing myself on the table as the room seemed to spin around me.

"Anyway, the whole conversation reminded me how much we used to love going to Chase's games. I miss it, Maddie. And I know you and your friends go to games all the time. I was wondering if maybe I could join you sometime?"

Panic zipped through my bloodstream. "Oh, to an Outlaws game?"

"Right! Wouldn't that be—"

"We should go to a Blizzard game. That would be—"

"No, those tickets are so expensive, and watching the pros isn't the same."

I struggled to breathe. "Well, let's talk about it. I actually need to—"

"I was looking at the schedule. I think there's a home game—"

A knock sounded at the front door. "Hey, Mom? There's someone at the door. Can I phone you back later?" Normally I'd be pissed at someone showing up at my apartment at eight ten in the morning on a Saturday, but right now, it was the perfect escape.

"Oh, sure. Promise you'll phone soon?"

"Yep. Promise. Love you, Mom."

The knocking started up again, more insistent this time. I dropped the phone back on the receiver and ran for the door. I flicked the dead bolt and turned the handle. *Damn it, if that was Garrett I was going to—*

The blood drained from my face.

Chase was out of breath, his sweatshirt sleeves shoved up to his elbows, hair damp and curling at the edges. His mouth parted as his eyes dropped, sliding over my braless torso and bare thighs.

My toes curled against the small patch of linoleum that was our entryway. I couldn't force myself to move. How was Chase Wilson standing on my doorstep? Why was he here? Where had he gotten my address? The questions jammed my head so full, all I could get out was, "Chase? It's Saturday."

He dragged his eyes back up to mine, planting his hands on his hips. "Yeah. Saturday."

I stared at him, crossing my arms over my chest as the cool morning air brushed over my skin making everything . . . perk up. "I—what—" And then it hit me. Saturday. "Shit," I hissed.

"There it is."

I pressed my fingers to my temple. Saturday. Axel had mentioned it last night at Ranchman's. He'd said his math professor held open office hours during the week but on the second Saturday of the month he was available in the morning and I shouldn't drink too much because he was hoping I'd be there, and I'd said, "For sure!" Then Axel had scribbled down the time and the room number and I'd shoved it in my purse then promptly forgotten about it because *Chase was walking in with freaking Melody Sanchez.*

"What time is it?" I spun in a circle, searching for a clock, but the microwave wasn't visible from the front door.

"Eight fifteen."

I spun back to Chase. "Is Axel already there?"

He nodded. "He searched my number in the staff directory. He tried your number and it was busy."

I groaned. "He woke you up? Wait—why is your personal number listed in the directory?"

"Kind of not the point right now."

"Right. I—Okay, give me five. I'll—" I exhaled in a rush, glancing down the street. "I had to park three blocks over last night. I think someone was having a party—"

"Just put some damn clothes on and get in." Chase pointed at his truck idling on the curb.

"Okay. Right." I slammed the door shut and ran to my room. Thankfully, my jeans were draped over the end of my bed. I pulled them on, then strapped on my bra and pulled a crewneck Douglas sweatshirt over my head. I stubbed the same toe on the way to the washroom, brushed my teeth through my watering eyes, and ran out the door.

CHAPTER
Twelve

THE CAB of Chase's truck was warmer than I expected. Or maybe that was just me with sweat beading at my temples and my skin buzzing from the morning chaos and the fact that I hadn't exactly planned on having a front-row seat to Chase Wilson before washing my face.

I adjusted my seatbelt, trying to place the smell. It was pleasant. Like peppermint gum and something that reminded me of my friend Corie's grandpa's garage. Old leather. Dry grass.

I'd never spent time in my own grandpa's garage, and I doubted it would've smelled the same if I had. Corie lived on a farm just outside of town. I went there after school almost every day after my dad passed. I hadn't thought about that in ages, and it made my eyes sting.

"You okay?" Chase adjusted his grip on the wheel as he pulled onto the main road.

I glanced over, realizing I'd been staring dead-eyed out the windshield. "Oh, yeah. Sorry." He gave me an odd look, and I turned my head. My breathing started to settle. My heart did not.

Outside, the streets of Calgary blurred past in streaks of

neutrals punctuated by bright spring green as new grass and leaves timidly peered out. Plants were smart to be reluctant here. Every year, there was a ninety percent chance we'd get a late frost and a fifty-fifty chance whether we'd get a snowstorm in July.

I blew out a breath, trying to wrap my head around what my mom had said on the phone. And the fact that Chase just saw me in my underwear. I guess it was only fair, considering. "We're even now." I folded my hands in my lap.

"Even how?"

"I saw you in your underwear in high school, and now you saw me." I thought if I acknowledged it, it wouldn't be as awkward.

"Oh. I wasn't—I didn't notice." Chase's cheeks reddened, and he swallowed hard.

I couldn't help it. I snorted. Thankfully, Chase laughed along with me, and the tension evaporated. Before it could get awkward again, I said, "I'm sorry I forgot about this."

Chase shrugged. "No worries."

My pulse quickened. "Why didn't you just do the meeting without me?" Without adrenaline flooding my bloodstream, I was thinking more rationally now, and Chase standing on my doorstep first thing in the morning didn't compute. Even if I had missed a meeting.

He draped his hand over the wheel as we stopped at a light. "Axel wanted you there." He fiddled with the heating vent. "And it's important to you, right?"

I shifted in the seat. It was important to me, but why would Chase care about that? He thought this whole committee was stupid and pointless. Which left only a couple of options for why he would've driven twenty minutes away from campus to pick me up. One, he cared about Axel. Two, even if he thought the committee was a ploy, he cared about his reputation and wanted to look good in front of Lamont and the others. Or three . . . he cared about me. Not *me* me, but my feelings about this particular situation. Based on what I saw last night, I was going with number two.

"I'm sorry I made you drive all the way out here. I promise I'll be more organized—"

"Why do you keep apologizing?" He pushed down on the gas.

"Because I should be more professional—"

"This is a volunteer assignment. You can do it however you want, and you've already done more than you committed to."

That . . . was true. Last Tuesday, I was sitting in his office going over numbers. Then the win and the image of him walking into Ranchman's with Melody Sanchez flashed in my head. It felt like a waste even though I knew that wasn't true. I wasn't doing it for Chase. I was doing it for the team, wasn't I?

"Thank you, by the way." Chase turned and drove past the sign welcoming us to the Douglas University campus. "Everything you said. It all worked."

And he took credit for it, I was sure.

He pulled into the lot behind the GRB Science Complex and swung into a faculty parking space. I pushed my door open as soon as the truck stopped moving. "Hey, you're the one who got Blakely on board."

His brows pinched, but he didn't say anything as I grabbed my bag and hopped down to the pavement. The campus was quiet. Unless there was a game that afternoon, Saturday mornings at Douglas meant empty sidewalks with only a few brave overachievers walking between the buildings. I would know since I was often one of them.

We crossed the quad and climbed the steps to the physics wing of the Coxeter Building. The fluorescent lights buzzed overhead, and it smelled like lemon cleaner. I wondered if Sharla finally convinced Rob to quit his janitorial job, otherwise, it very well could've been him cleaning these halls last night after Ranchman's.

Chase stopped outside Room 203. A plaque beside the door

read: Professor Ivan Hennings, Department of Applied Mathematics. Voices filtered through the door—Axel's low rumble and the professor's clipped accent.

"Ready?"

I nodded, not quite sure what would happen next. But then again, nobody knew. This type of student athlete intervention had never occurred at Douglas. I couldn't really do it wrong if it didn't exist in the first place.

Chase held the door for me, and I walked in. Professor Hennings barely looked up from his desk as he quizzed Axel on formulas. I sat next to Axel, who gave me a grin and a wave, and waited.

It didn't take long before Professor Hennings took a break. "I'm impressed. You have a better understanding of the application than I expected."

Axel gave me a wink. "It's coming along." He straightened and put his hands on the desk. "I hoped we could talk about extra credit for me to bring up my grade."

Professor Hennings interlaced his fingers. "I'm sure it will increase after the next unit test." He glanced at Chase. "But I'm guessing that if your coach is here, you're concerned about something beyond a math grade."

Axel ran a hand through his dark waves. "Yeah, no. Fer sure. I'm worried about ice time." He glanced up at Chase. "I'm working hard to bring this grade up, but I'd like to play with the team in the meantime."

Professor Hennings pushed his glasses up his nose. "Is it up to me?"

Chase nodded. "Partially. We're piloting a new program. Our academic advisors need to see that a plan is in place and that our players are willing to put in the work."

Hennings turned his attention back to Axel. "Is this the only class you're behind in?"

Axel shook his head. "I have an appointment with Professor Mills Monday."

"And your next game?"

"Exhibition Wednesday night. Then a tournament next week-end." Axel's knee bounced under the table.

It wasn't only about that game, and all three of us knew it. We had barely two weeks until the Canada West playoffs.

Chase stayed quiet, arms folded across his chest, letting Axel lead. When they finally wrapped up, Hennings laid out a very clear plan: Axel needed to pass his unit final next week. No makeup tests. No extensions. He'd be cleared to play on probation until then, but if he didn't pass? He was out.

As we left the office, Axel turned to me and, without warning, pulled me into a full-body bear hug. "Thanks, Maddie girl." He squeezed, and I laughed, pushing against his chest.

"You haven't passed yet."

He let go, his eyes dancing. "But I feel like I can." He smoothed my sweatshirt on my shoulders. "Appreciate ya." He dropped his hands and turned to Chase, clapping him on the back and steering him a few steps down the hall. Their voices dipped low.

My interest was instantly piqued, but I didn't want to seem like I was eavesdropping. I couldn't exactly leave since Chase was my ride, so I studied the announcement board like I was doing exam prep and strained to hear what they were saying.

"Thanks again, bud." Axel's voice was barely loud enough for me to make out something intelligible. " . . . money by next Friday."

My head tilted. *Money?* Chase said something I couldn't catch. Axel nodded and clapped him on the shoulder again. I stayed put until Axel walked down the hall in the opposite direction, and Chase turned back to me.

"Ready?"

I spun from the board, doing my best, "Who, me? I completely forgot you were there." If Chase saw through my acting, he didn't let on.

Back in the truck, that same warm, minty, familiar scent enveloped me.

"So." Chase ran his hands over the wheel, and the soft, brushing sound gave me goosebumps. It was like I had a processing disorder. Every piece of clothing or object he touched became an extension of my own body. "We should update Lamont about Axel," he continued. "Write up the plan and put it out to the committee."

I nodded. "I'll include Hennings's breakdown and tweak the academic support schedule for his exam prep."

We talked through the logistics and ran over the week's schedule with our study sessions. When there was nothing left to discuss, the cab fell into momentary silence.

Chase exhaled. "Well. Blakely's going to be thrilled."

Coach Blakely. Of course he'd be thrilled. He'd get all his players on the ice.

That comment dragged the last game to the forefront of my mind, and a tangle of yarn seemed to lodge behind my ribs. I pulled on the thread that said, "Chase is obviously going through something," or "He doesn't owe you anything, you offered to help," but that only tightened the knots.

No, he didn't owe me anything, and yes, he was probably emotionally stretched, but weren't we all? That wasn't an excuse. I was sick of giving people my answers and watching them ride off into the sunset.

"If you're free this week, would you want to go over numbers for the next away game?" Chase asked. "Clearwater's tough. I thought we could get ahead of their penalty kill—"

I turned to him, my eyes flashing. "Not free this week." I didn't expect him to be a mind reader in this moment, but asking me to help meant he was either desperate. Or oblivious. Or both.

Chase pulled up to the curb. "Did I say something—?"

"No." I shoved open the door and got out of the truck, that knotted ball starting to strangle me. Even in that moment, I knew the pressure building inside me wasn't only the numbers.

It wasn't even only Chase. It was years of me feeling taken advantage of. Tiny moments stockpiled over time. Sharing homework, saying yes to favours, doing the group project. Putting forth so much effort a thousand times over, and what did I have to show for it? Good grades? Now I was working my ass off to pad my resume for a scholarship and he wins the hockey game and waltzes into Ranchman's with Melody Sanchez?

Okay. So maybe it was more about Chase than I realized, which was why I didn't want to talk about it with him. I pressed a fist to my chest, trying to draw a full breath.

"Maddie, stop." Chase grabbed my elbow, turning me to face him. I hadn't realized he'd gotten out of the truck. "What did I say?"

"I really don't want to talk about this."

He nodded, his jaw working. "About what?"

Damn it. One sentence and I'd given away that there *was* something to talk about. Was it the discombobulating wake-up? The meeting with Axel? The smell of Chase's truck? I was the rational one. I didn't spin out of control and have emotional meltdowns.

I swallowed the lump in my throat. "I'm not feeling—"

"Does this have anything to do with the game? Or Melody? Because—"

I coughed. "Why would it have anything to do with Melody?"

Chase put his hands on his hips, splitting his jacket and exposing his fitted T-shirt. "You shot out of Ranchman's after we got there. And you looked pissed."

My mouth worked. "I—I had an early morning." I folded my arms, scrambling to get off my proverbial heels. "Why was Axel talking with you about money?" Chase frowned. Ha. Perfect. I doubled down. "He said he'd have the money for you—why? Some playoff bracket bet or something?"

"No. I don't bet money with students—"

"But you'll buy them a sandwich so they can make you look like a genius?"

Chase blinked.

I turned back to the door and dragged my keys from my pocket. "Sorry. I know that wasn't fair," I muttered as I shoved the door open and stepped inside. It wasn't a true statement. It was an emotional one.

I stared at my empty living room. Was this what it felt like to have your feelings hurt? Truly hurt? It sounded ridiculous, but I wasn't sure I'd ever experienced it, and none of it made any sense. *Why was I so upset over a stupid game?*

I rubbed my hand over my breastbone, trying to ease the pressure underneath. Footsteps sounded behind me.

"It's not fair. I asked for help and you said—"

"Yes! I know, I always say yes!" I whirled to face him. "I don't want to disappoint people, but then I'm the one who ends up sitting here disappointed!"

He stood silhouetted by the sunshine outside the door. "The Outlaws won. I thought that was the whole—"

I let out an exasperated growl, kicked off my shoes, and stalked toward the kitchen. Did I want credit? Did I want him to announce to the entire arena that their big win was because of numbers I crunched? No, that was ridiculous. It was the players who put in the time on the ice. The win wasn't because of me, so what did I want?

Chase followed me into the galley kitchen. I stood barefoot on the mat, coat still on, too wired to look at him. "It would've been nice to hear a 'thank you.'"

"Thank you," he snapped.

I gave him a snarky grin. "Wow. Feels good." I grabbed a plate from the cupboard and pulled my half loaf of bread from the bread box. Had I eaten this morning? No. That was definitely the problem.

When I took down the peanut butter and honey, Chase

moved in. "Here. Allow me. Apparently, I'm great at giving people sandwiches so they'll make me look like a genius."

"Chase—"

"No, seriously. What else could I get you to do for me?" He pulled open the drawers one at a time, searching for a knife. "I still have to submit my taxes—"

"Chase!" I grabbed his arms and wedged myself between him and the drawers. My breath caught when I looked up and realized our bodies were flush. "Stop it."

His muscles relaxed, and everything went still. "Did you think I told everyone those shift changes were my idea? Because I didn't."

"I don't even care. I'm just hungry and—"

Chase put a finger under my chin and tilted my face back up to look at him. "You stop it."

My heart beat in my throat. "Stop what?"

Chase's head dropped another inch, and my mouth went dry. "Mr. Wild knows you're the only reason I made it through Math 20, and Coach Blakely knows it was you who came up with the strategy for the game. The players do, too."

I nodded, but he didn't release my chin.

"Stop pretending like you don't care. You should care. You should get credit." Chase finally dropped his hand. "I wanted to thank you at Ranchman's, but you were a bat out of hell."

His words flowed through me like warm honey. How had he done that? Known exactly what I needed to hear?

"Well, this is interesting."

I jumped at the sound of Tash's voice, slipping out from between Chase and the countertop. She stared at us through the pass-through window above the kitchen sink.

My cheeks heated. "Hey! I'm so sorry. Did we wake you?"

Tash looked between the two of us. She was in a sports bra and baggy sweatpants. "No, you? It was definitely the mild beeping of my alarm clock and not the shouts of 'Stop it, no you stop it—'"

"Okay, I get it, I'm sorry." I pushed my hair behind my ear and spun, trying to find something to do with my hands.

"Who are you?" Tash asked.

"I—" Chase hesitated. "Was just leaving." Chase ducked his head and stepped back into the entry.

Tash followed, disappearing behind the wall. "I'm thinking not a student because you look like you have your shit together."

I scurried out behind him. "Tash—"

"You do look like a hockey player, though. With the arms. The stache."

"Tash, seriously." I gave Chase an apologetic look.

He gave a tight smile and opened the door. "Have a good weekend."

"Wait!" Tash's eyes widened. "Is this the guy? The one you were baking cookies for?"

"No!" I grimaced and hurried to close the door behind him as Chase stepped over the threshold. "Those were for the team!" I finished, too loudly. I turned to face my roommate, pressing my back against the door. "Really?"

Tash grinned at me. "That's him, isn't it? The coach, your brother, the guy you had the hots for in high school?"

I groaned. How much had I said while being lulled by the melancholy strains of Bush Y? Or Z? Or whatever the hell their name was? "You're an asshole."

She laughed. "Definitely. But you were just pressed up against a faculty member in the kitchen, so."

She had a point.

CHAPTER
Thirteen

THE STUDY ROOM in the North Centre still smelled like chalk and vending machine coffee, and I was grateful for it. I needed every ounce of intellectual stimuli available to do what I was about to do.

I'd done some thinking over the weekend and realized a few things about myself. First, I couldn't skip breakfast. Second, that blowup in Chase's truck? It was ninety percent about Melody Sanchez. Yes, I was annoyed that I hadn't gotten credit, but it wasn't about the academic props. It was that I wanted him to notice me.

It sounded pathetic, but that moment in the entryway? That knot in my throat? It unlocked something I didn't know about myself. It turned out, I wasn't immune to the immature longings that my friends always complained about. I wanted a guy to notice me for what I had to offer, just like they did, but what I brought to the table was my brain. I didn't have musical skills like Shar or a tiny, petite body with big boobs like Crystal—not saying that's the only thing she had to offer, it was just a very noticeable thing, considering the men constantly knocking on her door.

I wasn't going to pretend I wasn't beautiful. I was pretty, but

I was also different. As much as guys pretended they liked unknowns, it wasn't true. They liked to feel comfortable, safe, just like women did, and I was an unknown. Different skin, different hair. Add in high achievement, and that was a recipe for intimidation for most guys.

I thought I'd accepted that years ago and then re-accepted it when I broke up with Colin, but deep down? I wanted someone to notice me. I wanted to be loved for who I was and not for who someone wanted me to be. What better way to prove that I was worthy than for the guy I'd always been secretly obsessed with to want me? It was psychologically predictable.

I pushed open the door just before six, my heart tapping out its own nervous little rhythm in my chest. My bag slid off my shoulder as I stepped inside, and my heart sank. Tim and Nick were already there, hunched over their textbooks.

I walked in and set down the tray of chocolate-covered Rice Krispies treats I'd made. Probably another bid for acceptance and attention on my part, but I was taking baby steps.

Tim wolfed down the rest of his banana. "Eeeey! Maddie!" He waved me over to sit across from them.

Okay. I was hoping to catch Chase alone to get all of this off my chest, but it could wait. "Hey." I dropped into the chair.

Chase sat at the far table, brows furrowed, scribbling in a notebook. A calculator rested at his elbow, and a mess of game notes was spread across the table. He looked up and gave a small nod.

I smiled, then turned back to scan Tim's assignment. Something about probability distributions and binomial functions. I could do this in my sleep, so while I walked through the steps with Tim, my brain ran its own internal lecture series.

Planning 101. Your poetry response is due on Thursday. Right. I'd been avoiding that one. Not that I couldn't write it, but the poem we'd been assigned was . . . unsettling. I read it once and hadn't been able to go back to it.

The Rhodes applications open up in June with a September dead-

line. You need to start preparing your essays— I shut that one down straight out of the gates. I had to wait until this experiment was over anyway, so I wasn't going to focus on that until classes were out.

Communications 101. When you talk to Chase, say it how it is. He already knows you had a crush on him, it won't come as a surprise. He'll probably appreciate the honesty, and then none of this will be awkward anymore.

"Okay." I tapped Nick's page. "That's your mistake. You're squaring n, but you should only be squaring the variable."

He blinked. "You sure?"

I raised an eyebrow.

"Right. You're sure." He scratched it out.

Ten minutes later, both guys packed up, thanked me, and grabbed a treat.

Then it was just me and Chase.

I hid my balled fists under the table. "I need to talk to you about something." Better to get it over with.

Chase looked up. He was in a pale-green button-up shirt with the sleeves rolled. It brought out the flecks of tourmaline in his eyes, and that wasn't helping. Rip off the Band-Aid.

"I told you I had a crush on you. At Ranchman's."

Chase's eyebrows lifted in surprise. "You did."

"Well, I think my biology is still attracted to . . . your biology." His mouth quirked, and I swallowed hard. "Just a purely phys-ical thing that I can't control, and because of that, I think I've been trying to—" I paused, trying to catch my breath. "I wanted to impress you, I think, not you specifically, but really any guy."

"Okaaay."

I pressed my palms into the table like I was flattening a ball of dough. "Like I was helping other people in the hopes that you —or someone—would notice me and make me feel accepted. Worthwhile. You know?"

Chase blinked.

"Again, that's a me problem. So I was feeling used by you, but really I was trying to use you. As proof."

"That . . . you're lovable."

"Yeah, or like, hot or something. Because I'm smart, which I know isn't a thing—"

"It's a thing."

I scoffed, my cheeks so hot that I thought they might burst into flames. "Not a thing. Maybe for guys it is, but for girls it's better to be funny. Or . . . happy."

Chase fought a smile. "Happy?"

I nodded. "You know those girls."

"I do know those girls."

"Like—"

"Melody."

I wet my lips. "Exactly."

Chase leaned back in his chair, flipping his pen between his fingers. "You know that doesn't always mean they're happy. For real."

I shrugged. I didn't know because the only girl I knew like that was Sharla and she was indescribably happy. *Now*. I considered that thought. She hadn't been fully happy with Logan. "Maybe not, but they're more attractive."

Chase rubbed his chin. "Maybe."

I gave him a look. "Maybe? Those are the only girls you date."

An exhale of breath, a drop of his eyes, and that smile split his face. "You don't know who I date now."

"I mean—"

"I'm not dating Melody."

"Well. You met her after."

Chase gave me an amused look. "Yeah."

My heart sped. I leaned over to pull my binder out of my bag, then flipped to my literature section. "It doesn't matter, I already explained what was happening there, so I just wanted you to know. That's why I got weird." I grabbed a pen and flipped to the poem handed out in our last lecture.

The Fire Sermon from *The Waste Land* by T.S. Elliot. Barf.

"Because of the biology thing."

I glanced up. Chase stood next to my table. Pen behind his ear. Papers and calculator in his hand. He kicked out a chair and sat, spreading his work out next to mine.

"Right. But I'm working on that." I looked back at the poem, the words blurring in front of me.

"How?"

I chewed my lower lip. That was an excellent question. "By acknowledging it and saying it out loud."

"And that gets rid of it?"

Hell, no. I was starting to sweat. "Mmhmm."

"Huh. Well that's good to know."

I underlined the title on my page.

"Should've used that in high school."

I snorted. "Whatever. You got whoever you wanted. You didn't need to make anything less awkward."

Chase didn't answer right away. I moved on to underlining the poem, hoping he'd gone back to his work.

"Maybe I was looking for proof, too," he murmured.

The rush in my veins slowed to a deep, rhythmic pulse. I drew a breath and looked up. Chase's brow was furrowed. He was reading my poem.

"Don't—"

"This is about sex."

I pursed my lips, heat flashing up my neck. "Yep."

Chase made a face. "Terrible sex."

I laughed, then felt a swoop in my stomach when I realized that probably meant he knew the difference. What had Shar said that night she slept at my house? Good sex happened when you could talk about anything?

I stared down at the page.

"'The time is now propitious, as he guesses,

The meal is ended, she is bored and tired,
Endeavours to engage her in caresses
Which still are unreproved, if undesired,'" Chase read aloud. "So . . . the guy's a creep."

I nodded, my eyes still glued to the page. It was the next lines that did me in. *His vanity requires no response . . . one final patronizing kiss . . . Well, now that's done, and I'm glad it's over.*

"Hey, you alright?" Chase's hand dropped onto my shoulder.

I stiffened, blinking to clear the haze in my vision. "Sorry." Was I crying? In front of Chase Wilson? How embarrassing—

"Zero connection. They're both in their own worlds."

I froze, staring back at the page as something inside of me broke open. "Exactly." He was trapped in his selfishness, but she—she was trapped in her head. Not even noticing when the man left. Feeling nothing while he was there. And yes, the poem was talking about trauma, but that wasn't what gut-punched me. I'd been her with the guys I dated. I'd thought those words. I was always trapped in my head. So how was I supposed to let someone in when I couldn't even figure out how to escape myself?

Chase's hand still sat on my shoulder, and it didn't feel wrong. More like it belonged there. I stared at my notes. There were lines everywhere. Little comments in the margins. Arrows between stanzas. But no thesis. No opinion. No argument that didn't feel like peeling back skin.

I reached for Chase's game notes, but he pushed them out of the way. "Nope."

My head snapped up. "I was going to help—"

"No. You're not." He tapped the paper in front of me. "I'm going to help you write this response." He plucked the pen from my hand and started writing.

Carbuncular is a perfect name for this asshole because—

• • •

I laughed out loud and stole the pen back. "Thanks, but no thanks."

"I'm kidding." He tried to take it back, but I gripped the pen tight, and his hand circled around mine.

As I turned to get leverage, his hand slipped from my shoulder to my neck, and my head tilted back and—

My lips found his.

My arms went limp.

My soul may have left my body.

Because I, Madelyn Taylor, was kissing Coach Chase Wilson.

Fourteen

CHASE DIDN'T ONLY EXHALE when he smiled. He did it when he kissed, too. Besides that, everything about Chase in that moment was foreign—the feel of him, the taste of him. His mustache tickled my upper lip, and I half smiled as his mouth toyed with mine. My body felt suspended, like some unseen force was lifting me from my chair while simultaneously wrapping around every inch of me and squeezing tight.

The cap of the pen bit into my palm, but I barely noticed because Chase's hand slid to my wrist, up my arm, over my shoulder, and then settled around the base of my neck. His fingers brushed over my jumping pulse.

Somehow that touch was what allowed my brain to break through the haze. Well, that and the click of the doorknob.

My eyes flew open as Chase and I broke apart. His chair scraped against the floor as the pen flew out of my hand, landing at the other end of the table. I scrambled for it as the door pushed open, and Axel and Rory burst into the room.

"Hey," Rory cut short when he looked at me. Then his eyes shifted to Chase. "Everything okay?"

I nodded, holding up the pen. "Yep. Just clumsy."

His eyes narrowed a touch, but they barrelled in and set their bags down.

"I made flashcards," Rory announced proudly. He pulled a stack of note cards from the side pouch of his backpack. He waited for my response then repeated himself when I didn't immediately praise him. "Made flashcards like you suggested. To study for biology."

In my defence, I was seconds away from asphyxiation. I nodded, wetting my lips as I straightened my shirt and willed my lungs to expand. *I could still taste him*—the same hint of mint from his truck, and there was a slight tingle in my lips from whatever lip balm he had on.

I cleared my throat. "Well, hand them over. Let's get going."

I just kissed Chase Wilson. Or had he kissed me? It was like we were two ends of a magnet, and it had just . . . happened. I flipped my binder closed, since I couldn't focus on anything with Chase's sentence staring up at me, and got to work.

Axel and Rory stayed until five minutes before the study session time ended, at which point they completely devolved into mountain retreat planning while gathering as many Rice Krispies treats as their hands could hold.

"The house has seven bedrooms and a hot tub on the patio. It's going to be wicked, bud." Axel turned to me. "You can share a room with me, Maddie. Since we have to double up."

Chase made a sound in his throat.

I laughed, pretending not to notice. "Pretty sure Crystal already claimed me."

"Perfect. The more the merrier." He winked, and I rolled my eyes. I stuffed my binder back into my bag and was about to cover up the rest of the tray when I paused and held it out to Chase. "Do you want one before I go?"

Chase looked up at me, then glanced at Axel and Rory goofing off next to the door. It was a look that said, *We should talk about this*, but I wasn't ready to have that conversation—not when all I wanted to do was drop the tray of Rice Krispies on the tile and climb into his lap. I raised an eyebrow and pretended to lower the Saran Wrap. Chase's nostrils flared. He reached out a hand and snatched one.

"You ready for tomorrow's exhibition?" Axel asked.

Chase took a bite from the corner of his Rice Krispies treat. "I'm not the one who needs to be ready."

Rory put Axel in a headlock. "Gotta toughen up, impress that scout."

My eyes flared. "A scout?" I reacted before my thoughts had time to cycle back to the conversation we'd had a couple of weeks ago. Right. *Coach Wilson has a connection.* "Is the scout going to be at the game?" I asked, my heart falling a little.

Secretly, I'd enjoyed that Rob had been so occupied with preparations. Seeing Shar and Crystal together on campus every day after class had been a much-needed return to normalcy.

I covered the tray and backed away with Chase's eyes still locked on mine. Yes, it was cowardly, but I needed to think. There were reasons why making out with Chase in the study room wasn't a good idea, but I couldn't quite grasp them at that moment. I needed fresh air, and I needed to talk to Shar and Crystal.

I gave a small wave. "Okaaay. Well, good study session."

Rory yanked the door open, and Axel gave Chase a salute. "See you on the ice, bud."

Chase nodded once. "It'll be a rough one today, boys."

Rory shouted something that sounded like "Hell yeah!" but as it was a mix between a battle cry and a whoop, I couldn't make out the words exactly. I split off from the guys as we exited the North Centre. They went left to the Dome, and I went right to the east side of campus.

It had taken Shar all of three weeks before she gave up and slept almost exclusively at Rob's, but tonight, since the boys had practice, I was hoping I'd catch her at home. I had to talk to someone about what had just happened or I was going to burst.

I tried to replay the moment in my head—tried to catch each

second with clarity—but it was impossible. He was reading the poem, and then we were both grabbing for the pen, and then— It was like we were caught in a whirlpool, swirling closer and closer until there'd been nothing left to do but meet.

I adjusted the straps of my backpack. His hands had been on my notebook. His hands had been *on me.*

That made my stomach flip. I'd been honest with him, and it hadn't felt weird at all. He didn't make a big deal out of my admission. If anything, that conversation had lowered the strangeness. Even now, while I didn't want to have a post-game breakdown with him, it wasn't because I thought it would be awkward. It was because I didn't want to hear or say the thing that was sure to be said.

Chase's lips on mine didn't equal the proof I'd been seeking, not under these circumstances. There could have been a hundred reasons why it had happened—we were alone in a room together. Reading a poem about sex, albeit terrible sex. I'd just admitted I was still attracted to him, and Chase . . .

What he must be going through with his mom, with his job. I didn't tell him that I'd heard about any of it, and after that kiss, I wasn't sure I was going to. Those brief seconds may not have equalled proof, but if I left the kiss there, standing in time, then it could mean whatever I wanted it to, couldn't it?

It could mean Chase Wilson found me attractive. It could mean that even though I was a few years younger and he'd never noticed me when we were in high school, maybe something had changed.

It didn't have to mean that he was emotionally compromised and saw an easy, desperate target and decided to take advantage. You know, *if* thoughts like that were clawing their way into my head.

I clenched my jaw and crossed the street. The sun crept toward the horizon, but every day, it stayed up a few minutes longer than the last. I hadn't realized how much my soul was craving more light. I couldn't wait for our weekend getaway in the mountains. We'd initially talked about spring break, but with Canada West and then the potential for Nationals, the boys weren't willing to make any commitments between the two. They had to beg Blakely to give them those three days at all.

I turned up Sharla's walkway, climbed the steps, and knocked on the front door to the girls' house.

Shar's roommate swung the door open within seconds. "She's not here." I frowned, and she leaned against the moulding. "She has a performance tonight, I think?"

I deflated. Damn it, I'd completely forgotten. It wasn't that I was supposed to attend—her performance was across town—but that meant she wouldn't be back until late.

"Okay. Thank you."

"Do you want me to leave her a message?"

I shook my head. "All good. I'll catch her tomorrow."

I retraced my steps back to campus and found my Rabbit along the curb just south of the GRB Complex. Tomorrow night, Shar, Crystal, and I were getting together during the exhibition game since it was closed to anyone but team members and staff, and we couldn't attend. This memory could exist in my body for twenty-four hours without causing internal combustion, couldn't it? I could talk to Tash, but implosion seemed preferable.

———

The three of us locked ourselves away in Shar's room on Wednesday night, and before we could even settle on the bed, I said it out loud. "I kissed Chase."

And just like that, the bubble popped, and reality flooded in to fill the vacuum. Chase was a faculty member. What would happen to his job if anybody found out? What about my place on the committee? While it wasn't the only thing on my resume, it certainly made it more compelling. Especially if we found good results at the end of the semester. The write-up sounded less compelling when it included, "Oh, yeah, and I'm sleeping with the coach."

Not that we *were* sleeping together or even *would* sleep together. But my body had not been sated by one kiss in the study room. That curiosity, that fascination I had with Chase hadn't dissipated by feeling more of him. If anything, it had the opposite effect.

Crystal gave me a look. "Wait. You kissed who? Garrett?"

"No." I flopped down on Shar's bed and hissed, *"Coach Wilson."*

Shar and Crystal were the personification of deer in head-lights. "What? When?" They gathered around like children waiting for bedtime stories.

I told them everything, and they asked the same questions I had only just started asking myself.

"Yeah. No. I know. It can never happen again."

"I mean . . . it could happen again." Crystal played with the tassels on one of Shar's pillows.

"Would he get fired? It's not like he's *your* professor or coach," Shar asked.

I stared up at Shar's popcorn ceiling. "No. He's not, but it wouldn't look good."

They both nodded in agreement.

"Do you two want more than that?" Crystal asked.

"I don't know." I grabbed the pillow she was fiddling with and dropped it over my face. That was the truth. I knew how I felt around Chase, how I'd always felt around Chase, and that feeling was intoxicating. Especially when, for me, that sensation of everything slowing down, of the wheels inside my head grinding to a halt, didn't seem to happen with anyone or anything else. But did that mean I wanted *more* with him? I'd never gotten past the simple idea of him.

"I guess I always imagined you with some brainiac or something," Crystal said.

I pulled the pillow from my face with a look of horror. "Do you think I need more over-analysis in my life?"

She chortled. "No. I just meant someone who could match your smarts."

"Those guys are all nerds," Shar said, and I laughed.

"Not all of them."

Crystal leaned back on her arms, and the mattress jumped. "Remember that guy, Matt or Marty? Oh, it was Marty."

I knew exactly who she was talking about. He was a farm boy, a grad school student who wore Wranglers and looked more than good in them. "Okay. I take it back. They're all nerds or assholes." Marty had definitely been that. I went out with him once and spent the entire night listening to him refute every benign comment I made.

"At least you know smart guys do have the potential to be hot," Sharla teased.

"It's not like Chase isn't smart." I suddenly felt defensive. He might not have been good at math in high school, but he'd figured out how to get a bachelor's.

Crystal raised an eyebrow. "You tutored him when you were fourteen and he was seventeen."

"That says more about her than him." Shar got up and grabbed her hand lotion off the dresser. She took some and passed it around.

"But wouldn't it always feel, I don't know, lopsided?" Crystal asked.

Something twisted between my ribs.

Stuck.

Alone.

The words of the poem flooded my mind. *Well, now that's done, and I'm glad it's over . . .*

Shar put the lotion back and sat down on the foot of her bed. "Rob doesn't play violin, and that doesn't feel lopsided."

"But that's more of a skill, not the way your brain thinks," Crystal argued.

Shar's brows pinched. "I don't know if that's true. Anyone who's able to work hard enough to be excellent at something must have some level of intelligence. And more importantly, the drive and determination to make it happen."

I turned to my side and propped my head on my arm. "True. And then you have to worry about whether your priorities line up."

Shar nodded, chewing her lower lip. "Yeah. Relationships are terrifying. There are too many factors."

The feeling of Chase pressed against me in the kitchen, his hand on my neck, his lips on mine, jumped back onto centre stage. My brain was quiet in those moments, but afterward? "Or maybe we make them too complicated," I murmured.

Why did it matter if Chase was faculty and I was a student? It wasn't like I asked to be on the committee with him. And if anything, having him there only made me work harder. Why did it matter if he'd technically been my stepbrother for a bit? It wasn't like we were actually related by blood or that anything weird happened when he was at my house.

Why did I have to think about whether this was a smart decision or even a long-term one? Why couldn't I just give in to whatever this was and worry about the consequences later?

Said every teenager ever.

I was twenty-one, but I hadn't ever gone through a rebellious stage. Seemed inconvenient to jump into one now.

"It's probably a nonissue since Chase won't even be here next year."

My head snapped to Shar. "What?"

She stilled. "You didn't know that?"

My mouth worked. No. I didn't know that.

Crystal jumped in. "Wasn't he barely hired last semester?"

Shar held up a hand. "All I know is what Rob told me. He came in knowing it would be short-term. But I think the guys are a little bit sad about it. They really like him."

Footsteps sounded down the hall, along with the roll of deep bass and baritone voices. Shar looked at the clock in confusion just as her bedroom door burst open to reveal Rob and Axel.

Rob rushed in and scooped her off the bed. He lifted her into his arms and kissed her as her legs wrapped around his waist.

"Okay. Get a room," Crystal snarked.

Rob broke off the kiss and grinned at her. "I'd be happy to if you wanna get out."

Crystal rolled her eyes. "What's going on? I thought you had the game."

"It was just an exhibition. We didn't even split it into periods. Just played for about forty-five minutes until the scout had what he needed," Axel explained.

"So you're done?" Shar's smile widened.

Rob nodded. "Come home with me, babe."

"Oh, for the love." Crystal pushed off the bed.

I smothered a laugh as Shar shot us both an unapologetic look. I scooted to the edge of the bed, then yelped as Axel dropped onto the mattress next to me, giving me a double bounce. He laughed at the panic on my face. "Maddie girl, what are you doing this weekend? I—wait, don't answer that." Axel clamped a hand to my mouth. "Let me tell you what you should be doing."

I nodded, breathing in the scent of whatever soap he'd used in the showers. This oughtta be rich.

"We have a tournament this weekend in Clearwater, BC. My unit test is on Monday, and we won't get back until probably midnight on Sunday, eh, Rob?"

Rob nodded, finally releasing Shar's legs so she could stand. Axel dropped his hand from my mouth, and I rubbed my nose before I sneezed.

Axel turned back, grinning. "So come to the tournament with

us. I already talked to Coach Wilson. He said we'll have some time to study on the bus, Friday when we get there, and Saturday before our game. Then on the way back, too."

My eyes widened in surprise as warmth diffused through my chest. Chase was so wrong about this. Axel cared. Yes, maybe it was only because he wanted ice time, but that was something.

I fiddled with the pillow, trying to look casual. "You talked to Coach Wilson about this?"

Axel nodded. "Yeah. He thought it was a great idea."

"Did he now?" Crystal smirked.

My eyes flicked to Shar's. She knew what a sacrifice this was if I agreed. I never slept well away from my own bed. I had a nighttime routine and hotels messed with it.

"I'm going," she said, grinning at me as her teeth scraped over her bottom lip. *Very subtle.*

I dropped my eyes as my heart picked up speed. "I mean, I guess I could."

Axel actually celebrated, pulling me into his chest and squeezing tight. "Yes! I took a practice test today, and I failed it."

"You what?"

Axel scrubbed my head with his knuckles, then extricated himself as I shrieked and grabbed his beefy arm. "I'm sorry—sorry! I won't mess up your hair."

"How bad did you fail?"

He waved me off. "Does it matter?"

"Yes. It matters!"

"I'll pack the quiz and my stuff. We can look it over on Friday." Axel jumped up with a grin and pulled his shirt down. He made a heart with his hands and held it over his chest. "See you then, Maddie girl."

I rolled my eyes and worked to swallow the lump of nerves in my throat. Because while I was invested in helping him, Axel was definitely not the person I was thinking about seeing Friday.

"This is perfect!" Shar clapped her hands together. "We can share a room!"

"So you can keep an eye on her?" Crystal teased.

Rob looked between the three of us. "Is there something I'm missing?"

"No!" We answered in unison, and I stifled a groan.

Not suspicious at all.

Fifteen

I SHOWED up at the Dome Student parking lot Friday morning with my small suitcase and my pillow. Shar and the guys greeted me with hugs. We tried to get Crystal to come along for the weekend, too, but she had commitments she couldn't ditch on last minute. Plus, it was her brother's birthday, and we were all going to be together for the weekend after Canada West anyway.

A couple of the other guys' girlfriends were driving separately, but Shar and I were given VIP seats on the bus. If you could call them that. Technically, I was the only VIP, but when I expressed to Coach Blakely how I'd rather not be the only girl at a sausage party—not in those words—he agreed to let Shar ride with me instead of taking Rob's truck. She was more than grateful not to spend the gas money.

I scanned the lot as the driver loaded in the gear. Coach Blakely and the Outlaws' assistant coach, whom I didn't know, stood near the door of the bus. Blakely scribbled something on a clipboard.

"He's not here," Shar whispered.

"Obviously."

"I guess he's driving over on his own."

My heart slipped a little. What did I think, that we were going to sit together on the bus, hold hands, and have a heart-to-heart in the middle of the entire Outlaws team? I dragged in a breath then slowly released it.

"Have you talked with him?" Shar asked, keeping her voice low.

I shook my head. There hadn't been tutoring hours on Thursday since Chase had a conflict and the guys were getting ready for their tournament. I hadn't seen him since I walked out of the study room with my tray of Rice Krispies treats, which wasn't good for my head.

Did he regret it? Was he embarrassed? Or worse, was he going to pretend it never happened, and I was going to go the rest of my life wondering if I'd made the whole thing up?

At Blakely's signal, we loaded onto the bus. Axel saved me a seat since Shar was spoken for by Rob, and Rory dropped into the seat across the aisle. He may have failed his quiz, but at least we had specific concepts to work on and he wasn't lacking in enthusiasm. Rory came prepared, too. His flashcards were stuffed into the water bottle holder on his backpack.

Blakely introduced our driver, who elicited cheers from the guys when he told them he planned to play country hits the entire way to BC, and then we were off. The time went fast sitting with Axel and Rory, not only because we were going through problem sets and then working as a threesome to quiz each other on anatomy and musculature—they were both thrilled that they knew some answers that I didn't—but also because they brought snacks. All-dressed chips, fuzzy peaches, wine gums, and whack-a-Mack toffee. I could barely eat a full Teen Burger meal when we stopped at A&W for lunch.

Axel bought two full meals, brandishing a stack of cash as he sat down in our booth. "I'm flush, buds."

Rory shook his head. "Not even yours."

Axel grinned. "Until Coach Wilson gets to the hotel, it is."

My eyes narrowed. "That's for him?"

Axel nodded. "Yup. I owe him big time."

I speared two fries and a cheese curd with my fork as Shar and Rob sat down at the table across from us. "Why do you owe your coach?" I asked with some hesitation, not sure I wanted to know.

Axel exhaled. "Saved my ass. I owed rent and didn't have it."

I blinked at him. "He paid your rent?" Was that even allowed?

Axel shoved the cash back in his pocket, unwrapped his burger, and took a massive bite. "Half of it."

I chewed on that. "Wow." So . . . I felt a bit sheepish for accusing him of gambling with students. But why didn't he just tell me that?

We finished our lunch, and as we got back on the bus, I was headed back to my seat when Coach Blakely stopped me. "Madelyn, I was wondering if I could steal you for the next part of the drive?"

I pursed my lips to hide my shock. "Yes. Of course. What do you need?"

He motioned for me to sit next to him, then pulled out a spreadsheet. "Normally, I'd run this past Coach Wilson, but he's not here, and he made it very clear that you were the brains behind this analysis anyway."

My heart warmed. So Chase hadn't been making that up. "Sure. I'd be happy to take a look."

I wondered if this was the data Chase had been looking at on Tuesday. They had stats not only on the Outlaws from the last game but also from Clearwater. We analyzed the numbers at a high level, then dove into special teams and penalty-kill strategies. Clearwater was disciplined. They rarely got sent to the box, and while the Outlaws weren't especially chippy, we could expect five to ten minutes of penalty time based on our track record so far.

When Coach Blakely paused to pull out his water bottle and some black licorice, I mustered up the courage to ask, "So why isn't Coach Wilson here?" It was a natural question, considering I was sitting there helping with his job. I hoped he couldn't see the blush threatening to rise to my cheeks.

Coach Blakely popped a piece of licorice in his mouth. "He had a media appearance this morning. He probably won't get to the hotel much later than we will, but he couldn't leave until ten."

A media appearance? Chase had played for one, possibly two feeder teams, but that was at least a year or two ago. "Why would he be doing an appearance that isn't connected with the Outlaws? Is it something to do with his scout?"

Blakely shook his head. "Nope. He's doing an interview for Young Pucking Players. YPP. Heard of them?" I shook my head, and Blakely grinned. "It's a youth organization, started a couple of years ago by Alvin Bennett to help support players who are currently homeless or who may need to get out of a rough situation. Chase serves as their COO."

My mind was now exploding. First, rent money for Axel, and now this? Also, Chase knew Alvin Bennett? *The* Alvin Bennett? The soon-to-be NHL hall-of-famer who was all over the current Canadian Tire commercials? Not only that, Chase was only twenty-four, and he was serving as a COO?

This was not the Chase I knew in high school—the Chase who didn't show up for class or who laughed about waking up passed out in the back room of a Pizza Hut.

"It's a nonprofit volunteer position," Blakely continued, taking a swig from his water bottle.

"When does he have time for that?"

"He makes time. Had some kids over here at the rink after our six-to-one win the other night. Spent time with them on the ice. Let them meet some of the players."

My mind whirled back to Chase entering Ranchman's with Melody Sanchez. *He met me after.*

"Well, I won't keep you from your friends." Blakely patted a beefy hand on the stack of papers attached to his clipboard.

"You've really got a talent for this, Madeline. Have you considered going into coaching?"

If my jaw hadn't already been on the floor after hearing about Chase and Young Pucking Players, it would have dropped then. "Coaching? I've never played hockey."

"You don't have to play to be good with the numbers." Blakely gave me a smile. I sat there stunned for a moment, then pulled myself together and rose from my seat. Had he really just suggested I think about coaching hockey? Was it strange that the first person I wanted to tell was Chase?

"Thanks." I gave a smile, then moved down the aisle to my seat.

We arrived at the hotel just before four, which meant we had three hours to rest and relax before the guys needed to be at the rink to gear up and run an extended warm-up before their game at eight thirty. It was going to be a late night, especially if they won and we all ended up at the bar after. But at least their next game wasn't until two p.m. Saturday afternoon. Then if they won, they'd play the championship game Saturday night.

Shar and I went straight to our room and crashed. We didn't have to wake up that early, but talking nonstop on the bus was surprisingly exhausting. After sleeping and grabbing dinner at the hotel bar, we took the shuttle to the arena, where the guys were already on the ice. The Outlaws had been begging for a rematch against Clearwater since our Invitational, but we had to get through the Fraser Valley Lynx from Chilliwack first.

"Have we played them before?" I asked Shar as we settled into our seats.

She shook her head. "I don't think so."

I scanned their players, but it was hard to tell who would be our biggest threat when they were all seated on the ice, stretching. Their navy, silver, and deep forest green jerseys bordered on pretty. "I kind of want a shirt that looks like that." I pointed, and Shar laughed.

"Pretty sure you could find it at Northern Reflections."

After introductions and the national anthem, we finally got to puck drop. Our guys were fired up from the get-go. Strong on the forecheck and winning their puck battles.

Rob scored at the six-minute mark after a beautiful backdoor pass from Axel. They celebrated in the corner then skated back and tapped gloves with the rest of the guys on the bench. Rory scored late when Rob took a wrister from up top and the puck rebounded off Fraser Valley's goalie's stick. He was in position to snag the puck and flick it in, elevating over the goalie's pads and hitting top shelf.

When it was 2–0, I breathed a little easier. Our boys were dominant, controlled, and only gave the Lynx four power play minutes the whole game. Shar and I stood and cheered for the last minute and a half, then escaped the arena to wait for the guys at the small bar that shared a parking lot with the hotel.

While most of the guys opted for pizza instead of drinks, we still managed to stay out until one in the morning. The buzz from my beer had nearly worn off when Shar looked at me, bleary-eyed.

"Sleep."

I nodded. "Did you even drink tonight?" I asked as we dropped from our stools.

Shar shook her head then leaned over and planted a kiss on Rob's cheek. "I wasn't feeling great after the game."

"And we didn't even have a corn dog," I said. She grinned, walking with me to the door. I held it open for her. "While I'm thrilled that we get to be roomies, is there a reason you're not staying with Rob?"

She looped her thumbs in her back pockets. "Only that I'm an amazing girlfriend."

"To me or him?"

Her smile widened. "Both. No, I just didn't want to take away from this. It's his tournament with the guys. I want to be here, but I don't want to distract him."

We pushed out the doors and started across the parking lot. The night was warm and still. Shar's face pulled into an apologetic grimace. "Okay, since we're talking real, can I ask you a question, and promise you won't get mad?"

Did a question about our roommate situation constitute real talk? I laughed. "This is probably the best time since I'm still a little buzzed and haven't gotten to my post-beer sappy stage."

Shar sighed. "Aw, I love your post-beer sappy stage."

The parking lot light momentarily flooded over us before we passed back into shadow, the laughter and music from the bar fading behind us.

"Are you—" Sharla fiddled with her hands. "So I think I know the answer to this, but I just wanted to be sure." She chewed her lower lip. "Do you like men? Or—"

It took me a moment before I figured out where she was headed with this line of questioning. I gaped at her. "Shar, are you asking if I'm a lesbian?"

Sharla held up her hands. "Zero judgment. I just wondered because you said sex wasn't great with Colin, and you haven't dated anyone in the last, what, year and a half? Two years?"

I laughed out loud. "Oh my hell, I'm not a lesbian."

"Okay! I just wanted to tell you that if you were, it would be fine—"

"Do you think I would hide something like that from you?"

She laughed. "I don't know! Maybe you hadn't figured it out yet."

"And you thought now would be the moment—in a parking lot at a hockey tournament—when I'd suddenly realize, 'Oh! The reason penis sex wasn't great was because I don't like penises!'"

Shar grabbed onto my arm, trying to cover my mouth. "Shh! You just yelled 'penises' across the parking lot twice."

We both dissolved into a fit of snorts and giggles, pausing at the row of cars. It was quiet out, and it felt more appropriate to have this conversation in the dark before walking into the lobby of the hotel.

I wiped my eyes and lowered my voice. "Maybe I just haven't found the right penis yet."

Shar put a hand on her hip, pretending that was a very astute observation. "But, like, nobody? There aren't any guys that you have even the tiniest crush on?"

I blew out a breath. "I don't think I know how to have crushes." I paused a moment, then took that statement back. "No. That's not true. I think I know what a crush is. It's just that my body has decided to sabotage me and feel things only for men I can't have."

Shar smirked. "Coach Wilson?"

She said it like she was singing "Happy Birthday, Mr. President," and it was my turn to shush her.

She laughed and pulled away as I grabbed her arm. "There's nobody out here!"

"I know, but—!" I gestured back at the bar where the team could exit at any moment, then pulled the clip from my hair, shook out my curls, and swooped them back up in a twist, securing them again. "I just—it's like my body found his frequency back then . . . "

"And your antenna is broken? You can't switch from AM to FM?" Shar finished for me, continuing with the sound wave metaphor.

"If that's a gay joke—"

Shar chortled. "Maybe you just need to sleep with him and get it out of your system. He's like a crush blockage. Your mind does like doing things in order."

I groaned. "First of all, highly doubt that would ever happen. Second . . ." I allowed myself to consider it. To imagine Chase in front of me. All I could see was him exiting the washroom with that damn towel around his waist. I really wasn't very creative. "My high school self would lose her freaking mind."

"Babe, I hate to tell you, but you're still your high school self."

"I hope not."

Shar gripped my wrist. "No. I had this fantasy when I was sixteen that a super hot, ripped guy stepped out of my shower and wrapped himself in a baby-blue towel. So guess what colour of towels I bought for me and Rob?"

Okay. Maybe the towel thing was a common fantasy. I grinned. "Seriously?"

"Oh, yeah. And I make him stand there on the bath mat for as long as I want."

She stepped back, and I wrapped my arms around myself. "See, but that's the problem. I never quite got to the fantasizing stage. I stalled out at the *'Holy crap, I'm feeling things between my thighs'* stage."

Sharla grinned. "So you never once imagined something with Chase?"

I pondered that for a moment. No. I hadn't. I'd never plucked that image of him out of real life and dropped him into a story where we were together or . . . doing things. I was just mesmerized by him. That damn puzzle I couldn't figure out.

I blew out a breath. "I think the problem was—well, still is—"

"Right," Shar nodded her head. "Not enough data."

"Exactly." I thought of the spreadsheets on Coach Blakely's clipboard. It was so easy for me to see the patterns. But starting with a blank page—

"You could try collecting some information on your own, you know."

I balked. First the lesbian question, and now this? "I don't think I could do that."

Shar shrugged. "Well, you already said no to Garrett."

"Yeah, I know." I thought for a moment. "I can't even imagine—" I shook my head, my chest already starting to tighten. "I don't know. That feels terrifying, the idea of letting someone else see me like that, touch me like that." Yes, I'd slept with Colin, but those moments were more about survival than connection.

Shar's hands were suddenly on my shoulders. "Maddie. At some point you're going to need to let go."

I frowned. "Let go of what?"

"Everything. You hold it all so tightly, and I get it. You're good at what you do. You have a system. Everything is in order, and it works for you. But if you never let someone else take the wheel—"

"Letting someone else take the wheel would be dangerous. We would crash and die."

She grinned. "Letting someone else take the wheel means you can lie back and have a mind-blowing orgas—"

"Okay, so you're allowed to shout that across the parking lot, and I can't say penis?"

"Maddie, for the love!"

I laughed. "No. I get it. I hear you." And I did. Intimacy, connection, meant lowering those walls. Letting someone see all my inner workings. It wasn't that I didn't want to . . . I just couldn't figure out how.

"If you let somebody see past the grades and accolades and that brilliant mind of yours, they're going to love what they see."

I cocked my head to the side. "Shar. I don't think there *is* anything beyond that." It was a joke, but it also kind of wasn't.

"Oh, there's something there. And either you're going to figure it out gracefully, or you're going to have a shit storm of a meltdown at Oxford."

"I am not."

"What happens when school is over, Maddie? When you're working and you don't have that next test to study for or the next scholarship to win?"

"I—" My voice caught as the conversation with Chase snapped into my head. *Yeah. Well, my goal is to get them on the ice. Let them do the thing they love. After this, they're not going to have nearly as many opportunities.*

Suddenly, the next ten years of my life flashed in front of my eyes—getting the scholarship, studying, earning my degree, then maybe moving on for a master's or PhD, jumping from hoop to hoop to hoop, hopefully discovering something I was passionate about in the process. But would that happen if I couldn't even find something or someone to be passionate about now?

"What do you always tell Axel and Rory?" Shar asked.

I wet my lips. "That they need to do their laundry more than once a semester?"

She laughed. "The other thing."

I drew a breath. "That patterns of thinking change with practice."

"Exactly. So . . . You're really good at math. They're not, which means changing those patterns of thinking is going to take practice."

"So are you saying I need . . . practice?"

"Your words, not mine." She dropped her hands and adjusted her purse on her shoulder. "I just want you to be happy. Maybe you need a tutor, too."

Pressure built behind my eyes at the expression on her face. It was a different iteration of a look I knew in my bones. "You're looking at me like my mom right now."

"I'm not—" Sharla sniffed. "How about a good friend. And I'm not the one leaving, by the way."

I deflated a little. "I get it. I'm broken, and you need to fix me while you still have time."

A smile split her face. "It's more like I want you to stop depriving the male species of that sweet, sweet ass."

I threw my head back and laughed, almost stumbling over the parking block behind me. "Perfect. Well, I've got my homework. Find someone willing to tutor me in relationships and physical intimacy—"

"That'll be easy."

"—who doesn't make me want to throw up in my mouth."

"Okay. Maybe a slightly harder sell."

"Who isn't Chase Wilson. Because apparently, he's the only one my body knows how to notice at the moment."

"Right. Same frequency and—"

We both jumped as the slam of a car door sounded behind us. My head snapped to the left, and my stomach lurched like I was suddenly dangling at the top of the Drop of Doom.

Chase Wilson stood on the other side of his truck, and his passenger window was open.

CHAPTER
Sixteen

IF I THOUGHT Shar and Crystal were deer in headlights the other night in Shar's apartment, it was nothing compared to the two of us. A bulldozer could have been bearing down on us, and neither of us would have flinched.

My mind did the math.

No cars or trucks had pulled in or out of that parking lot since Shar and I had left the bar. He'd been sitting there the whole time. Three cars down. And Shar and I had *not* been whispering. Had he heard that last sentence? *Had he heard me yell penis sex?* I couldn't decide which was worse.

I wanted to die. I wanted to bury my head in the sand like an emu or ostrich—if that was something they actually did and not just another lie spread by Saturday morning cartoons.

What exactly had I said? Why had I opted to end with that closing statement? Had I referenced him since we were closer to the bar? Strike that final addition, and the rest of it would have been embarrassing but salvageable. But this?

"Sharla. Maddie." Chase coughed at the end of my name, then folded his arms only to think better of it and drop his hands on the hood of his truck. His jaw tensed, and he wouldn't meet my eyes.

Oh, *damn it.*

"I'm just going to—" Sharla slowly backed away, and I shot her a glare that said, *If you dare leave me alone right now, you're dead to me.* She mouthed, *"I'm sorry?"* Then turned and speed walked to the lobby.

That little skank.

I turned back to Chase, my cheeks burning. Hell, he looked good. A long-sleeved heather-grey T-shirt. His hair no longer combed like it had been at the game.

I had no other choice but to go on the offensive. "Were you just sitting in your car? Who does that?"

He rounded the hood, and I took a step back. "I was going to come into the bar, but then I got stuck on a phone call."

"At one in the morning?" What the hell time was it, even? I had no idea.

His jaw ticked again. "Yeah."

My curiosity spiked, but embarrassment overrode any potential questions. "How much of that did you hear?" I didn't want the answer, but I had to know.

He shrugged. "All of it, I guess."

"*All of it?* You didn't think to alert us to your presence?"

"I did."

I scoffed. "After you listened to all of it."

He took a step closer. "Yeah. I know that was a dick move, but I couldn't—" He ran a hand through his hair. "I couldn't stop."

Couldn't stop. What kind of excuse was that? My eyes burned. This was why I didn't open up to people. Why I didn't say out loud my deepest, darkest fears. "Well, I hope it was entertaining." I turned on my heel and started after Sharla.

Chase's footsteps sounded on the pavement behind me. "I have a biology problem, too."

I froze and looked over my shoulder. "What?"

"The biology thing or whatever the hell you were saying in the study room."

Nothing he said computed. "With Rory?"

"No." He let out an exasperated sigh. "The thing you were saying. About me. That you were trying to fix or get over."

My heart picked up speed. The biology thing. Ohhhh. *My biology in response to his.* That's what he was talking about.

Chase glanced sheepishly back at the bar, then walked forward and stopped in front of me. He shoved his hand in his pocket, searching for something. He pulled out a thin white card. My heart stalled.

"I heard you were looking for a tutor."

The swoop in my lower belly made my vision darken at the edges. Was he—did he just—

"Do you—?" He bit his lip and looked away, muttering something that sounded a lot like *"shit"* under his breath. When he turned back, his eyes locked on mine. "I'm not your professor."

"No." I shook my head.

"I'm not your coach."

I shook my head again.

"I'm not your brother."

"Correct."

"And you don't answer to me on the committee."

That was true. We were partnered up, but I reported to Lamont.

"Is there anything else that makes you feel like I'm in a position of power over you?"

I blinked. "No?"

"Say it more definitely if you mean it, Maddie."

That was part of the problem, wasn't it? I didn't view him as Coach Wilson. I viewed him as Chase. *Hot Chase.* Chase, who had been in my shower naked. Chase, who leaned against lockers. Chase, whose shirt rose a little above the waistband of his jeans when he reached for a water glass.

I shook my head. "No." It was the honest truth.

He handed me the key card. I took it with trembling fingers. "Since I apparently suck at poetry responses, maybe this is something I'd be better at . . . helping with." He wet his lips. "Room 413."

He hesitated another moment, then stalked past me.

I stood there. Speechless. *Chase Wilson just handed me his room key. Chase Wilson—* I whirled. "Chase won't you—how are you going to get in?"

He turned back, and the corner of his mouth lifted. "I have two keys, Maddie."

Right. Two keys. I only had one because Sharla had the other, which meant he had his own room. Of course, he had his own room.

I started to hyperventilate. "Like, right now?"

His nostrils flared. "Your study schedule is up to you, I guess." He took a step backward, momentarily bleached in the parking lot spotlight, then turned and crossed through the circular drive for check-in, disappearing behind the sliding doors.

I waited until my body remembered how to breathe then hurried inside. I scanned the empty lobby, forgetting which direction the elevators were. When my brain rebooted, I strode past the check-in desk and turned left, then stood in front of the elevator bank a moment before pressing the button.

I couldn't do this. Just show up at his room and—what? My heart punched a staccato rhythm against my ribs.

No. He wasn't my professor or my coach. And no, I didn't think he held some leverage over me. But there were so many reasons why this was a terrible, if not an irresponsible, idea.

The elevator doors opened, and I stepped inside. I hit the "three" for my floor.

It was past one thirty in the morning. Chase just overheard me talking about how I wanted him, and I had entertained the idea of an intimacy tutor with Sharla. Clearly, we were not thinking straight. I needed to go back to my room, get a good night's sleep, and wake up to study with Rory and Axel at eleven.

The elevator rose. I flicked Chase's card between my fingers.

If the team or Coach Blakely saw me entering his room, if anyone on the committee got wind of something going on between us—or my mom? No. The whole thing would be disastrous. Plus, he was apparently leaving at the end of the semester and—

The elevator slowed. It dinged as the doors opened. I willed my feet to move, but they stayed planted, rooted to the spot.

That last thought rolled through my head like a marble. *He was leaving at the end of the semester.*

My pulse kicked, and my mouth went dry. Right now, we weren't on campus, and we weren't even in Alberta. I wasn't on University time. None of the university staff was here now, and Chase wouldn't have given me his key if he thought there was any chance that someone would see me entering. Maybe he was on a different floor from everybody else?

The door started to close, and heat flashed in my middle.

I reached out and smacked my hand against the number four.

CHAPTER
Seventeen

I STOOD in front of Room 413, my skin buzzing. He'd given me the key, but was I supposed to knock before walking in? Should I have gone to my room and freshened up? No, because then Shar would've asked questions and—damn it, Shar was going to think I was still in the parking lot. I had to at least tell her—

The door opened, and I clutched the key card like a rosary.

Chase stepped back, pulling the door wide. "Were you leaving?"

"How did you know I was here?"

"I heard the elevator ding and checked."

He heard the ding? I glanced over my shoulder. That meant the walls were thin. Not that I thought we would, or that I would—

The elevator dinged again, and I launched myself into his room, flattening myself against the wall as he closed the door. "Sorry. I didn't want anyone to see me."

Chase leaned back against the door, folding his arms over his chest. "Am I that embarrassing to you?"

I blew out a puff of air, and then just like it had in the study room, the dam to my thoughts opened. "We kissed."

Chase nodded gravely. "We did."

"We didn't talk about it."

He ran a hand over the back of his neck. "Did you want to talk about it? Because you bolted—"

"I know. I didn't want to talk about it then."

"But you do, now?"

I nodded. "I have to know. Are you doing this because I'm—" My throat worked. Because I'm a total nerd and don't know anything about sex and look totally desperate? Pathetic? "I know about your mom," I blurted. Chase's eyes widened, but I didn't let him interject. "My mom said something about her being in prison, and I swear, I had no idea." I walked into the room and sat on the end of the bed. "She said you took this job because your dad had some connection, which I'm sure you hated since I know how you feel about your dad. Or felt, I guess. And then Sharla said you might be leaving at the end of the semester, so I know you might not be in the best place right now."

Chase leaned against the TV stand. "Well. That's—"

"And you already know how I felt in high school, and now that you eavesdropped—"

"I wasn't trying to eavesdrop."

"Well, you weren't *not* trying."

He sighed, giving me that. "You already gave me the gist of all that the other day."

"Not all of it. And not like that."

Chase pushed off the wooden stand and crossed to sit next to me on the bed. "I didn't give you that card so we could have sex." He pressed his hands into his knees. "Not that I wouldn't want to. You do have—"

"If you say a sweet, sweet ass, I'm going to walk out right now."

Chase laughed. "I was going to say you have a beautiful body."

I blinked. That was . . . unexpectedly kind. Gentle. Not at all like the comments I got from guys on campus. Was this what happened? Men grew up between twenty-one and twenty-four?

"What you said. In the parking lot. I get that."

I swallowed. "Which part?"

He turned his head to look at me. "When you said you didn't know if there was anything else underneath."

His eyes were the same beautiful blue, but there was a sadness there, rippling under the surface. Had I noticed that before?

"You say you idolized me, but I don't think that's true." He leaned back, resting on his elbows. "You always called me out on my shit."

"Math shit. That was the only kind of shit."

He laughed. "That's not true. Remember when you told me I needed to go to bed early because I had a tryout the next day?"

My face screwed up in confusion. "No. When did I—"

"You did it all the time. I'd be there after school, you'd be making your peanut butter and honey sandwich, and you'd ask me what I was doing that week. I'd tell you I had practice or a tournament or whatever, and then you'd ask if I needed food or if I was getting enough sleep. Then you'd tell me not to be an idiot and party all weekend, or that I looked better in grey instead of black, or—"

"Chase. That was me rambling because I didn't know how to talk to you."

He stared up at the ceiling. "I know. But it made me feel like someone cared." His tongue flicked over his lips. "It's why I came back on Saturday mornings. I liked seeing you." He turned, his eyes wide. "Not that I—I didn't think about you like that. You were younger than me, and I never—"

I laughed. "Trust me. If anyone was the perv in our weird little world, it was me."

He watched me smooth the hem of my shirt, then smiled when I met his gaze. "When I saw you in the stands and then at Ranchman's—"

"You saw me before Ranchman's?"

He nodded. "I saw you at every game."

Okay. That was . . . information.

"Every time I saw you, it was like something released in my chest. Like—" His expression tightened as he searched for the words. "It sounds stupid because it's not like we ever talked after I left, but it felt like I still knew you. And as you just outlined, my life is a bit shit right now. So that felt good."

I gaped at him. "Your life is not shit."

"You don't have to—"

"No, I'm serious." I spun to face him, crossing my legs under me. "You finished school. You've got a coaching job. Yeah, your family sucks, but that's not your life, Chase. You left and actually made something of yourself."

He gave a sardonic laugh. "I failed at the one thing I was good at."

"What, hockey?"

"Yeah. Hockey."

"Chase, there were, what, fifty or sixty thousand kids playing hockey when you were? All trying to make it? The WHL takes a hundred and fifty, maybe, and then from there—"

"I know math makes you feel better, Maddie, but my brain doesn't work like that." He folded an arm behind his head and lay back. "I had a shot. I blew it."

"Or you were good enough to get a damn shot."

He shrugged. I twirled his key card in my hand then dropped it on his stomach. "So why did you give me this?"

He met my eyes but didn't speak for a moment. When he did, his voice was low. "Because I'm lonely. And I think you are, too."

I swallowed, dropping my gaze. "So . . . what? We just talk?"

Chase's mouth twitched. "Or study."

My cheeks heated. "I don't even know what that would look like."

He picked up the key and reached across the bed, setting it on the nightstand. "That's okay. Because I do."

. . .

———

I lay on the bed as Chase turned out the lights. "Is this really necessary?"

"Yep. You're an overthinker. You need less stimuli."

I snorted. "Very scientific." It was kind of adorable that he was taking this seriously. "But the problem isn't in what I can see. It's in my head."

The lights flicked off, and I held my breath, trying to figure out where he was. The mattress moved, and he shifted to sit next to me. "Are you the tutor here or am I?"

I blew out a shaky breath. "I thought you said you were only good at hockey."

"I lied. I'm also excellent at jumping into stupid shit I shouldn't because I don't overthink it."

"Like right now?"

"Right. That enough proof for you?"

It was. Surprisingly. I didn't think I'd jumped into anything. Not even a pool. I always dangled my legs over the edge and then, maybe, fifteen minutes later, I'd lower myself in. Chase on the other hand had jumped off the gym roof into the back of a dump truck filled with old foam from the gymnastics centre when it changed locations.

"So what are you—"

"Nope. No questions." Chase's hand caught my wrist, and I sucked in a breath. "If you catch yourself trying to figure something out, just focus on what you feel."

"But—"

"Trust me, Maddie."

My breathing came in quick bursts as he flipped my hand and drew his fingers over the inside of my arm. "We're going to start small. All you have to do is focus on this touch. If any other thought comes in your head, say, 'no thank you' and refocus."

"I'll try."

His fingers trailed over the sensitive skin on the inside of my elbow, then up to the sleeve of my shirt before turning around and retracing their path. He found my wrist, my palm, then played with the ring around my finger. My brows pinched. The last person I wanted to be thinking of right now was my dad.

His other hand held mine. Was he watching me? Could he see better than I could somehow? Did he enjoy touching me, or —? *No, thank you.* I focused back on his fingers, now looping in slow, lazy circles.

"Do you like this?" he asked.

"Yes." It was true. I did like it. But I was also aching for him to touch more of me.

"Where else do you want me to touch?" he asked, as if he were reading my mind. "Don't think. Just say it."

"My stomach." Heat flashed in my face. "I'm sorry, I shouldn't—"

"That's a perfect answer," he murmured, and that heat turned molten as Chase's fingers left my hand and reached for my shirt. Normally, this was where I would shut down. Where my skin would go cold and I'd grit my teeth and nod and say I liked it when really, I was spiralling. Hard. Was my skin soft? Was my stomach flabby? Did he like what he saw? What were my hands doing? I probably looked like a zombie. Was I supposed to be touching him?

"No, thank you."

Chase's hand froze. "Do you—"

"No! Sorry, I was saying it. To my thoughts." My face screwed up with embarrassment, but before I could apologize again, Chase's lips brushed my cheek.

"You're so good at this already."

Then his hand was back at the hem of my shirt. He lifted

before I could process what just happened. Was he . . . complimenting me? On making a complete fool of myself?

"You're beautiful, Maddie. You don't need to worry so much about what men think." I gasped as his hand flattened over my stomach. "But maybe they've just never told you, so I'll give you some examples." He moved over my skin, his fingers rising and falling over my ribs. "Your skin looks silky, and now I can say officially that it feels better than it looks, but it's so smooth and golden."

The mattress shifted, and by the angle of his arm, I could tell he was lying on his stomach.

"And your hips, how they curve into your waist. It's like a—" his breath tickled my skin, making it prickle with gooseflesh. "What do you call it? A parabola?"

Okay. He got major points for that one. I couldn't keep my hand on the quilt for a second longer. I lifted it, feeling for him. When I found his shoulder, I moved up until my fingers were in his hair. My exhale shook as his hand curled around my waist and his lips brushed my stomach. "Thinking anymore?"

"Hm." It was more a whimper than a word, and Chase smiled against my skin.

"You'll have to try that again. I couldn't hear you."

"No," I said, breathless. Again, it was the truth. Somehow, my world had shrunk. Everything beyond this cocoon where he and I existed had faded, leaving only the heat of his hand, the moisture from his breath cooling on my skin.

He pressed up, moving further up the bed. My hand followed, still splayed through his hair. "Then this was a successful lesson." He settled next to me on his side and pulled my shirt down, then draped his arm over me.

I opened my eyes even though it was still pitch black and I couldn't see anything. I wanted to thank him, but the words felt final, and I wasn't ready for this to end. "Can we just lie here a minute?" I whispered.

He nodded against my hand, then settled in on the pillow

next to me, and my arm found residence in the space between his shoulder and jaw as I turned to face him. He slipped his leg between mine and pulled me closer. I shut my eyes, curling my other arm into my chest as Chase's hand left my waist to run over the knuckles of my spine.

I drew in a long breath, exhaled, then drew another, barely catching his, "Goodnight, Maddie girl," before I dropped under.

Eighteen

"I PROMISE, I didn't sleep with him," I hissed. The stands were packed for the final Saturday night. The Outlaws had made easy work of the team from Prince Rupert that afternoon, and now they were in the championship game.

Shar didn't look convinced. "You say that, but I see the way you're looking at him."

"I'm just . . . looking."

"Uh-huh."

I'd already filled her in when I snuck back to our room that morning. She was skeptical then, too.

I nudged her with my elbow. "It was totally innocent, and, by the way, this was all your idea."

She unwrapped a cinnamon bun from the concession stand then licked the icing off her finger. "I am pretty proud of that, actually."

"You should be."

"I didn't think you'd actually do it."

I smiled, watching the warm-up skate and allowing my eyes to flit to the bench every few seconds where Chase, Blakely, and Assistant Coach Kaplan—I'd finally gotten his name—stood discussing something.

Shar and I hadn't gotten much time to talk since Tim and Bear's girlfriends had been with us most of the day. But right now, they were still out in the hall buying snacks.

"I think I get it now," I whispered. "I can see why people would be a little obsessed with sex."

Sharla gave me an amused smile. "And you said nothing happened."

I laughed. "No, exactly. We didn't even kiss, but it's like . . . I don't know. I can't stop thinking about it."

Sharla handed me a piece of her cinnamon roll. "Just don't get too attached."

I scoffed. "Okay, that's not fair. First you tell me to study—"

"I didn't think it would be with Chase! You said, "Not Coach Wilson," remember?"

"You said, 'Maybe you should sleep with him and get it out of your system.'"

"I was kidding!" she hissed, then winced. "Kind of. But I didn't think about the fact that you'd probably get so emotionally attached. He treats you like you're supposed to be treated, and you're like a baby chick who's imprinted."

I rolled my eyes. "I felt that way before last night."

"That's true." She pulled off another strip of frosted cinnamon goodness. "I feel better about that."

The arena lights dimmed as the anthem started, and I rose with the crowd.

Pressure the left side. Disrupt their top line's breakout. Exploit the weak-side rotation on the penalty kill.

We had a plan, and now all we needed to do was execute.

Have you thought about coaching? Blakely's question popped into my head, and though I'd dismissed it the first time, now it had a bit of sticking power. Was that even something women did? Was it possible to run numbers for a team? Do the analytics? I made a note to research that when we got back to Douglas. Not that I would consider going that direction, but it was interesting.

The Outlaws had prepped for this game, and from the first puck drop, it showed. Our guys came out flying—tight forecheck, crisp passes, smart rotations. Bear neutralized number 17's rushes twice in the opening period, using his body like a wall. Axel, who'd been inconsistent through fall semester, was skating with total confidence.

"Did you see that redirect?" Shar yelled, jumping halfway out of her seat as Rory tipped a blue-line shot and sent it screaming past the goalie's blocker. "That's one of yours, right?"

I grinned. "We moved Rory up to screen on the power play. That goalie gives up high rebounds."

They were only down 1-0, but at the start of the second, Clearwater shifted into desperation mode. They leaned into heavy hits and tried to force turnovers in the neutral zone. They battled it out, but the scoreboard didn't change.

Sharla disappeared to go to the washroom for a bit in the third. Something wasn't agreeing with her stomach, but she returned just in time to see Tim make an exceptional save on a backdoor shot.

The entire third period felt like a knife fight in a snowstorm. Blakely started double-shifting Axel and Rob, and Clearwater was gasping by the fifteen-minute mark. But then a loose puck bounced off a shin pad, Number 17 caught a breakaway, and it was a tie game.

"Are you kidding me?" Shar groaned, burying her face in her scarf.

"They're losing coverage off the draw," I said, half to myself. "We need to slow the pace."

Chase must've seen it too because during the next whistle, he pulled Nick aside. The next line out dumped the puck instead of carrying it, forcing Clearwater to regroup. Maddeningly simple and effective. We got at least four solid shots on goal but couldn't finish.

The buzzer blared with the score still tied 1-1.

Overtime.

"They've got this," Shar whispered, squeezing my hand.

I nodded, my head starting to spin. What if Rob and Axel were too stretched? What if Axel started second-guessing himself? What if—?"

No, thank you.

I focused on the feel of the chilled arena air. Sharla's hand clasped around mine. The solid bench under my thighs, and suddenly I was back in my body. Present.

Maddeningly simple and effective.

I stared at the bench as the boys filed out of the tunnel, willing Chase to look up. It took a minute or two, but then his eyes lifted. When they stopped on me, I gave him a huge smile and a thumbs-up.

"Is that a—is he blushing?" Sharla teased.

"As if you can see that from here."

The puck dropped for overtime, and the tension in the arena crystallized. This was the home team, and we, as Outlaws fans, were in the minority.

The Outlaws played it smart, keeping their shifts short, never letting Clearwater control pace for more than a few strides. Bear was gassed, bent over his stick on the bench. Axel took a heavy hit and looked a little rattled. But Rob—Rob was a different animal in sudden death.

"He wants this," Shar murmured.

You could see it in every push of his legs. He circled high in the zone, eyes scanning like a sniper, waiting for that one seam to open.

I saw it the second he did.

Rory forced a turnover at centre ice and fed it through a narrow gap, perfectly timed. Rob caught the puck on his backhand, dragged it around the defenceman, and snapped it just under the bar—far side, blocker high.

The arena groaned, and we tried not to be asses with our tiny celebration, but Shar screamed loud enough to make my eardrum twitch.

Rob dropped to one knee, arms spread wide, and the rest of the bench spilled over the boards to swarm him. The Clearwater players circled back to their bench, and I wasn't uncompassionate. It sucked losing at home. We had plenty of experience with that.

"Holy shit. They're going to nationals, I just know it!" Shar bounced on her toes.

The team formed a line to shake hands, and Chase stood at the end. He leaned in to say something to Rob, who was beaming, sweat-soaked and wild-eyed. And then, almost like he felt my gaze, he looked up to the stands.

This time, he didn't drop his eyes or grin. He just held up the papers on his clipboard, pointed at them, then pointed at me. *You*, he mouthed, and everything inside me stalled.

Shar nudged me. "I think he's a little impressed."

I blinked back the tears welling in my eyes. "I don't know about that."

"Just own it, Maddie. And write the hell out of that essay for the Rhodes." She threw her arms around me, and my heart felt like it was going to burst. Maybe I didn't know exactly what lay beneath my constant analyses, but it felt damn good to see that it was good for something. That I could help people and use it for more than just pulling out A's on tests.

"C'mon, let's get down there!" Sharla yanked me toward the stairs.

I had to hand it to Clearwater. Even though they lost, their team stood at attention as the trophy was presented and our boys whooped and smacked their sticks against the ice. The teams intermingled, passing around compliments and congratulations.

Shar and I screamed ourselves hoarse with Kelsey and Emily, Bear and Tim's girlfriends. Twenty minutes later, we leaned against the concrete wall near the arena's main doors, waiting as the players filed out with their sticks and bags slung over their shoulders.

Shar rubbed her gloved hands together. "Kelsey found a bar five minutes from here that supposedly does poutine nachos and karaoke."

I laughed. "That sounds deeply unholy."

"She said there's a neon moose."

Kelsey nodded excitedly, holding up a flyer with the name "The Tipsy Bullwinkle" headlining the top of it.

"Clearly, we have no choice."

The doors ahead of us opened wide, and the Outlaws spilled into the lobby, clean-faced, shaggy haired, and cocky. The smell of cologne followed them like a weather system. Rob spotted Shar and rushed forward, scooping her into a hug.

Rory grinned at me as he passed, then veered off to meet one of the Clearwater girls he'd been eyeing from the ice. Atta boy. Tim and Rob were still buzzing from Rob's overtime goal, shouting something about getting a timestamp tattooed above his ass cheek.

Then Chase stepped out with the coaches, his team jacket slung over his arm. Blakely and Kaplan flanked him, both looking too tired to function. Kaplan made a beeline for the shuttle while Blakely scanned the crowd and nodded at Axel.

"You boys coming out?" Axel asked, cradling his stick across both shoulders like a baseball bat.

Blakely grunted. "My bones are creaking."

"You need a little oil to grease the hinges, then, eh?" Rory teased.

Blakely waved him off, heading after Kaplan, and all eyes turned to Chase.

He hesitated, just for a second. "I've got an early wake-up call, bud."

Axel frowned. "How early?"

"Planning to leave around four thirty. Need to be back in Calgary by the afternoon."

Right. He hadn't come on the bus with us. My chest seemed to hollow out.

We hadn't made a plan—I hadn't *said* anything—but I'd been thinking about going up to his room tonight. I'd imagined, actually fantasized, about his hand tracing lazy lines on my skin. About his voice in the dark. But if he was leaving that early, maybe that wasn't what he wanted. Then Chase looked over before clearing his throat, "I'm mostly packed. Should have plenty of time for a good sleep."

My heart sped. Plenty of time.

I tucked my hands into my coat pockets and tried not to smile like an idiot.

"Next time, then," Rory said with a grin, slapping Chase on the back.

He grinned. "Good game out there, boys."

As he walked to the shuttle, I turned to Shar. "I think I'm going to head back."

She tried to keep a serious expression but failed miserably. "You seemed really tired during the game."

"Yeah. Exhausted."

Rob scoffed. "Wait, you're not coming out?"

Axel threw up his hands. "Maddie girl—"

Shar shook her head and silenced them. "Nope! You will not pressure her. She's been helping you all weekend and deserves to cozy up and relax."

Axel grunted. "But we were going to do Endless Love."

"I'll do it with you, bud." Rory sidled up next to him, pulling the blonde he'd just met along with him.

They were going to have a blast, no doubt. But I already knew where I was going.

And for the first time I could remember, I didn't overthink it.

CHAPTER

Nineteen

I INSERTED the key in the slot, but before I could reach for the handle, the door cracked open. Chase stood there, backlit by the soft lamplight, wearing grey sweats and a black T-shirt that clung to his chest.

"Do you just stand there, watching through the peephole?"

He grinned. "Hi."

"Hi." My nerves melted as I walked in, and Chase leaned in, dropping a kiss on my cheek.

Ugh. How did he do this to me so effortlessly? "That was nice."

"I liked it." He brushed his hand over my lower back as I slipped off my shoes.

The room was tidy. His bag was zipped and leaning against the dresser, his jacket folded on the desk chair. I tugged off my coat and draped it over the armchair then unhooked my purse and set it carefully beside it.

"Congrats on the win." I turned, sliding my hands in the back pockets of my jeans. "And thank you."

"For what?"

"You know what." I pursed my lips, working to keep my smile from exploding over my face. That moment he looked up at me from the ice and pointed at his clipboard replayed in my head. "You made me feel like I was a part of it."

"You are a part of it." He crossed to the mini fridge, pulled out two bottles of water, and tossed one to me. Thankfully, I caught it.

I glanced at his packed bag, and something in my chest twinged. When we were back in Calgary, back at Douglas . . .

"You're quiet." He leaned his shoulder against the wall.

I twisted the cap on my water bottle. "You're leaving early."

"Yeah." He looked at the floor then back up. "I have a thing tomorrow afternoon."

"A thing?" I took a sip of water and sat down on the edge of the bed.

He nodded and drew a breath, considering. "I'm listed as my mother's next of kin. So I have to meet with her parole officer. Discuss a support plan."

That landed like a punch to my gut. "I'm so sorry."

His jaw twitched. "Nothing to be sorry about. Just life."

"Chase—"

"Honestly, I have you to thank for that, too."

My brows furrowed as he pushed off the wall and swivelled the office chair to face me, then sat. "I said no. The first time they contacted me."

"Understandable."

He gripped the armrests. "When I saw her after she went in, she blamed everyone else. She didn't want to get sober. Didn't think she was the problem."

I did the math in my head. Seven years, my mom had said. If she was getting out now, Chase would've been sixteen when she went in. The fallout would've been happening when he lived with us.

"I gave up on her. Didn't have any desire to be there when she got out. But then something you said, when you were talking about Axel and Rory, made me rethink everything. 'Maybe they just need one person to believe they can be more than what they are.'" He shrugged. "I don't know if she's ready to change, but she doesn't have anyone but me."

I twisted the cap from my bottle between my fingers. "You shouldn't have to be that for your mom, Chase. She should've been that for you."

He leaned back in the chair. "Yeah. I know."

"Can I ask you something?" My pulse rushed.

"Sure."

"Can I . . . touch you this time?" I forced myself to look at him even though I knew my cheeks were stained pink.

His lips parted. "I'm fine, Maddie. I don't—"

"No, it's not about that." It was kind of about that, but I'd been considering asking him since that afternoon, before I knew about his meeting with the parole officer. "I've never done that before, and when you asked me what I wanted last night— I guess I've never thought about that much, either. And then this popped into my head, so I thought—"

"Sure." Chase's chest lifted and fell in quick succession.

"I won't stay long. I know you have to leave."

"You can stay as long as you want." Chase set his water on the desk, then stood. "How do you . . . where do you want me?" He looked at the bed, then looked away. His fingers trembled.

"You're nervous." I didn't mean to call him out, but it was comforting. To see I wasn't the only one.

He breathed a laugh. "Not nervous. Just adrenaline."

I grinned. "Excited, then." He looked at me through his lashes, and a flash of heat hit me square in my middle. "Lie down." I pointed at the bed, right where I'd been the night before. I set down my water bottle then moved toward the lamp.

I hesitated. "Can I leave it on?"

He dropped onto the bed and propped himself up with the pillows. "Seems hardly fair."

"Hey, that was your rule last night, not mine."

His mouth quirked. "It's your study plan."

I grinned. "The light stays on." I took a step toward him. "But you have to close your eyes. That makes me nervous." I pointed at him watching me.

"Again. Hardly fair."

I shrugged unapologetically, and he chuckled. When his eyes were closed, I climbed onto the bed and kneeled next to him. For a moment, I just looked. Staring at all the parts of him that I wanted to inspect but couldn't without looking like a psychopath in public.

I leaned over, starting with the line of his jaw. "You shaved."

"I did."

I played with the corner of his mustache, and he grinned. "When did this start?"

"It was a joke last fall with my friends."

"Friends from . . ."

"The Hitmen."

I tried not to get all jittery. It wasn't a secret that he'd played pro hockey. "And you know Alvin Bennett."

Chase's eyes blinked open. "How do you know that?"

I put my hand over his eyes, forcing them closed again. "Blakely told me. About your non-profit. And I heard about you paying half of Axel's rent." I traced my fingers down his forearm, the warmth of his skin seeping into my fingertips. "Why didn't you tell me?"

"You were pissed. You're a little scary when you're pissed."

I laughed and pushed up his sleeve, revealing a pale scar that curved near his elbow. His bicep flexed under my touch. "Did you get this in a fight?"

"Bench press. Bad spotter."

I let my hand travel up over his shoulder and to his chest, pressing against the solid muscle. His heartbeat thudded against my palm. Fast. "Why did you lend Axel the money?"

I traced the line between his abs, then skimmed the waistband of his jeans before sliding my fingers under his shirt. His quick intake of breath sent a thrill down my spine.

"You're asking me to think. And that's a little hard right now."

I grinned. The idea of him enjoying this—of him feeling the way I'd felt last night—made me feel powerful. Sexy. "Sorry. You can tell me later."

He caught my hand with his, holding it against his stomach, his T-shirt stuck between us. "I lived out of my truck. For about six months."

"What?"

Chase kept his eyes closed, his brow furrowed. "I didn't tell my coaches. I didn't want to seem weak." His Adam's apple bobbed. "I eventually found a place, but it was expensive in BC, and I didn't have any skills. I started working at the garage. That made enough for me to pay rent, but it never felt easy."

Puzzle pieces tumbled into place one after the other. Chase fixing my Rabbit. Volunteering with YPP. Helping Axel. All of it made sense.

And I couldn't sit there and only touch him with one hand.

I lifted from the mattress and threw my leg over his waist, settling my thighs against his hips. I slid my other hand beneath his shirt and lifted it, drinking in the sight of his stomach and chest. He was thicker now, more filled out, and I liked it. A lot.

Without thinking, I curled over him, tossing my curls to one side and dropped my lips to the dip between his pecs. He didn't have much chest hair, and I wondered if he shaved.

I kissed him again and again, rolling his shirt up centimetre by centimetre. And it wasn't about whether I was doing it right. I kissed him because I wanted him to know that he was good. That I was sorry he had to live like that. I wanted to pull him into my arms and hold him, but since he was nearly twice my size, this was the best I could do.

Chase lifted his arms and pulled his shirt over his head, then reached for mine. I dipped my head so he could pull it off, sucking in a breath as his hands splayed across my bare back, catching on my bra strap.

Yeah. I was done touching him slowly.

I curled my hands under his arms and pulled myself flush against him, then kissed him. Lights flashed behind my eyes as we came together, and I pulled back, our lips barely touching as I worked to catch my breath. When I was mostly sure I wasn't going to pass out, I pressed in, pulling his lower lip between mine.

Where was this coming from? I'd never kissed anyone like this, never been the one to instigate or take charge. But it felt so natural with Chase. There was no performance, no proving myself. Just simple want. Curiosity.

I slipped my tongue past his lips, and his fingertips pressed into my back, pulling me hard against him. Everything was quiet and loud all at once. The hum in my ears. The pulse in my throat. The low, rough sound Chase made when I shifted my weight and felt him react beneath me.

Chase looped his hand in my hair and tugged my head to the side, kissing down my jaw, my neck.

I pulled my hands out from underneath him, needing to touch him, to—

He rolled, taking me with him, and caged me against the bed. His weight dropped over me, and I gasped.

"Did I hurt you?" he rasped.

I didn't answer, just wrapped my legs over his and pulled his lips to mine. "Chase."

"Maddie."

I arched into him, curling my fingers into his back, needing to be closer, desperate for—

A knock exploded against the door, and I yelped. We froze, our chests heaving.

Another knock. Louder this time. "Coach Wilson?" Blakely's voice was unmistakable. "You decent?"

Chase cursed under his breath and dropped his head, then pulled himself off me, adjusting his pants. I searched for my shirt, but he was already walking to the door. I dropped to the floor, hiding behind the bed.

The door clicked. "Yeah?"

"Hey, coach. Ah . . . sorry to bother you when you were . . . sleeping."

"Mmhmm."

I stuffed my fist against my mouth to keep from laughing.

Blakely cleared his throat. "I know it's late, but there's a player in the lobby. Currently with Vancouver. He played at the invitational and wanted to have a word. Since you're leaving in the morning—"

"Right. Yeah. I can come down in a minute."

My heart thudded in my throat. I swallowed hard. Rational thought slowly formed through the haze of the last fifteen minutes. What was I doing? Had I come up here knowing it would go this far? If Blakely wouldn't have come to the door, would I have stopped? *Did I want to stop?*

The door clicked shut. I waited until I heard his footsteps returning, then peeked out from my hiding spot.

Chase stood at the foot of the bed. He ran a hand over his face. He noted the hesitation in my face instantly. "You okay?"

I nodded, tucking my hair behind my ears. "You have to go."

He blew out a frustrated breath. "Just for a minute."

I looked at the clock. It was already past ten. "You have to get up early." I pushed up from the floor and finally found my shirt between the bed and the nightstand.

"Maddie—"

"It's fine." I kept my eyes lowered and pulled my shirt over my head.

Then Chase was there behind me, pulling the fabric down as I turned. "What are you thinking?"

I gave him a small smile, my eyes stinging. "That this has been . . . the best weekend I've had in a long time."

Chase smoothed my hair, tucking my curls behind my ear. "But?"

"But now we're going back home. Where I'm going to be a

student again. And you're going to still be a faculty member." He pressed his lips together and gave a small nod. "And I'm going to be gone for the—"

"You're not sharing a room with Axel, are you?"

I laughed. "No. Why? Are you jealous?"

His jaw ticked. "I don't like it when he calls you Maddie girl."

My smile widened. "What else don't you like?" I couldn't get enough of this, but it certainly wasn't helping the situation.

"If he could stop feeling you up every time you study with him, that'd be great."

I stifled a laugh. I wanted to push him back on the bed and pick up where we left off, and that realization sobered me. We only had a few weeks.

I shoved my hands in my pockets so I didn't reach for him. "What do you want?"

He looked away, then dragged a hand over his jaw. "I don't *want* any more, Maddie."

I frowned. While I hadn't expected him to drop to one knee and declare, *"You! All I want is you!"* I also hadn't expected that. "What do you mean?"

He leaned back on the desk. "Wanting doesn't make a difference. It either is or it isn't."

The words landed like a slap. It took me a minute, but I could see the truth in them. At the same time— "Why try then? Why work for anything if any possibility is acceptable?"

"I didn't say it was acceptable."

That sadness in his eyes returned, and I didn't need to ask any other questions to understand. Chase had fought for what he wanted and lost. He'd pushed through incredible struggles to play hockey professionally, and now it was taken from him.

I thought about the Rhodes, about my academic dreams, and Shar's comment in the parking lot. Was this where we all were headed? Had we all bought into the idea that if we worked hard enough, dreamed big enough, then someday we'd get where we wanted to go, but really, most of us would stop short?

"When do you submit your application?" Chase asked.

"End of summer." Again, he didn't have to say it.

He nodded. "And you're going to study abroad." From the second Chase had opened that door to Coach Blakely, my brain had been running behind the scenes doing the damn math.

Rate of emotional freefall in Chase's gravity: approximately 9.8 m/s². Time left in the semester: seven weeks, give or take. Probability of Chase staying on campus: close to zero, given the way he was talking, which meant I didn't even have to take into account my own potential moving date to know that the probability of heartbreak was at least 87%. Margin of error: +/- 4% depending on how vivid that makeout session remained in my brain. Standard deviation of rational thought: skyrocketing.

Chase tugged at my waist, curving his hand around my neck and pulling my head to rest on his chest.

And just like that, the next number surfaced.

Probability of me falling in love with Chase Wilson if this continued: 100%.

Probability of surviving it when we inevitably broke things off?

Approaching zero.

I didn't have to think about the repercussions to his job or my opportunities with the committee or Douglas. Those just piled onto the already insurmountable data.

Chase didn't want any more, but I still did. I wasn't ready to accept defeat yet. "You should go," I murmured.

He pulled back and cupped my face in his hands. We both knew I wouldn't be there when he got back.

CHAPTER
Twenty

THE SUITCASE LAY UNZIPPED on my bed, my potential clothing choices folded in neat stacks next to it. I'd pulled out options, and now I only had to narrow it down. A task that should be simple, but knowing me, would take at least half an hour.

I glanced at Chase's Hitmen hoodie draped over my chair. Apparently, he lent it to Nick over the weekend, and Coach Blakely handed it to me on the bus. Our committee meeting was Monday, and their practice wasn't until Tuesday, so he wondered if I could get it back to him.

I planned to take it. But somehow it got left here instead.

I walked over and picked it up, holding it to my nose. Even though Nick had worn it, it still smelled like Chase. I'd have to give it back eventually, but it wouldn't hurt anyone if I forgot for another week.

I dropped it back on the chair and went back to packing. This week had been a lot, and I was so ready for a break. Ready to be away from Douglas where everything made me think of Chase.

We endured the seven-hour bus ride home, but somehow I slept worse in my own bed than I had in the hotel in Clearwater. Then came the committee meeting. Chase and I sat side-by-side at the long table in the registrar's conference room, pretending we were professional and definitely not buzzing from the proximity to one another.

He barely looked at me the whole meeting, but when Lamont went on a long tangent about documenting test results, he reached beneath the table without even glancing over and hooked his pinky around mine.

The entire left side of my body short-circuited. I didn't write another note because I refused to pull my hand away.

We didn't talk about it because study hours had been cancelled for the week since testing was done for the break. Axel crushed his unit final Monday afternoon with an eighty-five, and I couldn't have been more proud.

I shoved my black bikini into the suitcase, and was on my way to the washroom to grab my travel toiletries when someone knocked. My heart lurched. I wasn't expecting anyone and Tash wasn't home, which meant—

I padded barefoot to the door and flung it open. My face fell. "Mom?"

She stood there in a light denim jacket. Her curls were swept up in a bun that had started to fall, and she held a bakery bag in one hand. "Surprise!"

I worked to recover, forcing a smile to my face. "What are you doing here?" I stepped out and embraced her. "Did we— Did I forget we made plans?"

She pushed past me and dropped the bag on the kitchen counter. "Nope, but we talked about me seeing a Douglas game. You've been so hard to pin down lately, I figured I'd surprise you."

A Douglas game. Right. On the phone. The day Chase had shown up at my door and seen me in my T-shirt and underwear. I closed the door as she turned to face me.

"I looked at the schedule and saw it was the Canada West tournament and the first game is here. I assume you're going."

"I am, but—"

"Perfect! We can go together, and then maybe I could take you to dinner? I brought banana chocolate chip muffins you can keep for breakfast." She pointed at the bag on the counter.

I let out a breath and stopped fighting it. "Sure. That would be great."

The energy in the Douglas Dome was electric. Packed stands, the sharp clink of cowbells, and the steady hum of excited chatter. It was rare that Douglas got to host a game of the championships, but because of the last few weeks, the Outlaws were the highest seed in this match up.

"Are these players all your friends?" Mom shouted, leaning in so I could hear her over the buzz of the crowd. She looked unreasonably delighted, clutching her hot chocolate, her lipstick already smudged on the rim.

I thanked Shar profusely for changing our seats for the night. It was no easy task since she was sure changing anything would end their streak. I'd convinced her by reminding her that we'd sat on that bench for the whole first half of the season with mixed results. It wasn't our good luck charm. She decided it was our matching scarves instead.

"Is that him? Your boyfriend?" Mom asked Shar.

She nodded with a proud smile. "That's him."

"You both have one more year?"

"Yep. We'll all graduate the same time as Maddie." She threw her arms around me and Crystal.

My mom gave us an "Awww! You're adorable!" look, and I silently apologized to my friends with shoulder squeezes. "You're so lucky to have such good friends. I wish I could've gone to University. Well, technically I attended for a semester . . . "

Mom went on about her experience, and I was glad to let her regale us with tales of her past. That meant she wasn't scanning the bench and possibly noticing that there was a familiar face there in a button-up shirt, holding a clipboard.

From this vantage point, it was hard to see his features, especially since his head was bowed much of the time. Once the game started, we'd hopefully be home free.

We chatted until puck drop, then cheered as the Outlaws won the first face off against Kamloops.

"This is way better than I expected," Mom commented five minutes into the first. "They hit hard, and they're so fast."

I laughed and took a sip of my pop. "Did you think this was going to look like PeeWee?"

My mom continued on like she'd never seen a game before, but truly, maybe it had been close to five years. Since Chase left, I realized. She commented on the goalie's reflexes, Rob's handling, and the kid from the opposing team who had a mullet and apparently reminded her of her high school boyfriend.

I'd almost forgotten all about Chase until midway through the second period, during a particularly long delay.

She leaned in toward the ice, her eyes narrowing like a hawk that just spotted prey. "Is that—?"

"Ohmygosh I love it when he does that." I pointed at the other end of the ice where Tim, our goalie, seemed to be feathering a nest right outside the blue paint.

"That's Chase Wilson." Mom's voice was sharp. She turned to look at me. "Maddie. That's Chase–"

"I know." I blew out a breath, trying not to cower as she stared at me with the intensity of the sun through a magnifying glass.

"We talked on the phone. I told you he'd accepted a job, and you didn't say anything."

I winced. "You were talking about other things, I didn't want to interrupt."

She gave me the full eyeball. "Why wouldn't you have said something when I showed up? Or anytime in the last month? I —" She sucked in a breath and looked at me, the wheels turning in her head. If I was good at assessing data, my mom was an expert at reading me.

Shit. I shouldn't have kept Chase a secret. I should've casually mentioned that I'd seen him on campus, because she knew I came to the games. She knew there was no way I wouldn't have noticed him, which meant I was keeping it from her purposefully, which I was.

"Are you two *involved?*" She lowered her voice on the last word. "Or did he—when he lived with us, did you ever—"

"Mom, stop. No."

"Why else wouldn't you say something? We had an entire conversation—"

"Can we not do this right now?" I hissed, grateful that Crystal and Shar were pretending they hadn't heard anything, but the people behind us weren't so accommodating. They watched us like we were their personal time out entertainment. I pointed back to the ice. "It's starting. Can we talk about this after?"

I scanned the bench as the Outlaws took to the ice. Chase stood with his arms crossed, his clipboard tucked under one elbow. He looked focused. Strong. Sexy as hell.

"Have you seen him? Talked with him?"

I swallowed, my mouth so dry it hurt. "A little."

Mom leaned back on the bench, shaking her head. "I can't believe you didn't tell me."

I searched for an excuse and latched onto the first thing I could think of. I lowered my voice as the ref dropped the puck in the Outlaw's zone. "I didn't want to hurt you, Mom. That time was rough. I figured it was better to let it stay in the past."

Her expression softened a little. "Well, I wouldn't want to see his father again, but Chase . . . I always had a soft spot for him."

That made two of us.

Thankfully, she dropped back into hockey talk for the next two periods. She yelled at the refs when Rory went down hard after a blindside check and curled in on himself near the boards. He skated off under his own power, but his shoulder hung limp.

Shar covered her mouth. "Is that a separated shoulder?"

"Let's hope not." I muttered. Maybe he'd just hit his funny bone.

Chase adjusted. Blakely pulled Bear off the third line and shifted him to fill Rory's minutes. Chase double-shifted Rob on power plays and ran tight defensive pairings.

I silently cheered him on. The smile was back on Mom's face when the Outlaws entered the third with a 3-2 lead. The third period was the longest twenty minutes of my life. Kamloops pressed. The Outlaws held. Rob blocked a shot with his leg. Tim laid out to stop a cross-crease pass. Blakely looked like he was aging in real time.

And then—finally, with twelve seconds left—Bear cleared the puck out of their zone. The buzzer sounded. The crowd exploded, and the Outlaws poured over the bench, gloves and sticks flying as they wrapped their arms around each other in pure exultation.

Mom stood and cheered, and I almost thought she'd forgotten about Chase in all the excitement until she turned to me and said, "Do we wait in the lobby to see Chase or do we need to go down there?" She pointed at the tunnel.

I stifled a groan. I wasn't getting out of this. "C'mon."

I opted to take her to the lower hallway, not fully to the locker room because I didn't want witnesses for this, but at least we'd have a bit more privacy. Now I just had to hope Chase exited where we could see him. After a few players trickled out, heading for the stairs, the door further up the hall opened and Chase stepped out.

"Chase!" Mom called. He paused midstep and turned. At first he looked confused, but then his eyes met mine and his expression shifted. His shoulders dropped a touch, and he started toward us.

He gave me a questioning look as he got closer. I tried to communicate telepathically that I'd prefer if he took on his office persona and pretended he didn't remember my last name, but instead he threw out his arms and pulled my mother into a big hug.

She grunted as he squeezed the air out of her.

"What are you doing here?"

Mom looked like she'd just stepped off a merry-go-round when Chase stepped back. Her cheeks were flushed as she quickly smoothed her hair. "Well, I wanted to see a game, but Maddie didn't tell me you were coaching. I would've come sooner had I known."

Chase stepped back and smiled. "How have you been?"

"I could ask the same of you. I heard you'd gotten a job but didn't know it was here at Douglas."

Chase stiffened, and I knew exactly what he was thinking. How did she know he got a job? I didn't want to tell him the answer.

"Well, glad you could make it to the game. Did Maddie tell you we've been working on a—"

"I didn't," I cut in. "No, I didn't tell her about how you and Coach Blakely have been working on a new player support program. But I think it's great."

Chase raised an eyebrow. "You'll have to fill her in."

"I will." I coughed. "I think she'd find it interesting." The last thing I wanted to tell my mom was that I'd been working with Chase for weeks or that I had anything to do with running hockey stats. While she knew next to nothing about my major or the classes I was taking, she was always quick to remind me to focus. I highly doubted she'd find shot percentages or shift probabilities a good use of my time.

Blakely exited the locker room, looked both ways down the hall, then started our way when he spotted us. "Chase, are you —" He slowed when he saw me standing next to my mom. I sent up a silent prayer that he'd snag Chase and this whole interaction would be over.

"Maddie, good to see you. Is this . . . ?" He paused, probably recognizing that he didn't want to guess wrong on this rela-tionship.

"My mother," I finished for him, and he exhaled, holding out a hand.

"So nice to meet you. We've loved getting to know Maddie better this semester."

My mom's brow pinched, and I cleared my throat. "I'm sure you have plenty of work to do before you get home tonight." I grabbed my mom's arm, turning her toward the stairs.

"Thanks for coming, and Maddie, thanks for returning Coach Wilson's sweatshirt the other night."

I froze. Coach Blakely stood with his hands on his hips, smiling like he was proud that he'd remembered that. My eyes flicked to Chase's.

His lips twitched. "Yes, thanks for that. It's one of my favourites."

My heart could've synced with a hummingbird's wings. "Mm. No problem." *Damn it.* Chase knew I hadn't returned it, which meant he was probably envisioning me wrapping myself in it before bed each night. Which wasn't as far from the truth as I'd like. I wasn't wearing it, but I also wasn't not sniffing it every time I walked into my room.

Chase dragged his eyes from mine back to my mom. "It was great seeing you again."

"You, too. Congrats on the win tonight." She smiled, and I hurried her down the hall before anything else could come out of Coach Blakely's mouth.

Twenty-One

MY MOTHER and I talked in the parking lot for over a half hour, but I couldn't give her a satisfactory explanation for why I hadn't said anything about Chase.

Finally, I'd been forced to admit that I had a crush on him in high school. Embarrassment was finally a motivation she was willing to accept. That meant our conversations were likely far from over on that topic, but at least they were on hiatus.

Shar, Crystal, and I couldn't find a way to make the rest of the games for Canada West, and they weren't being broadcast. That meant we waited at Shar's after each game for Rob to call, and when all we heard was a roar over the phone on Friday night, we screamed and danced around Shar's apartment until her roommate threatened to call the cops.

The boys were exhausted Saturday morning, but we were going to have the weekend in Banff together before they started preparations for Nationals in two weeks. They had an automatic bid with five other teams around the country and would enter one of the round robin pools. Only the winner of the pool would advance to the finals, so they had to be on their game right from the get go.

Rob's truck sat idling when I arrived, exhaust curling into the chilly morning air. Axel tossed his duffel bag into the truck bed, sporting a backward hat and a six pack of pop under his arm. "My contribution."

Coach Blakely had been crystal clear. We could celebrate this weekend, but there was no drinking. The guys knew they had to be in tip-top shape next week, so none of them even thought about breaking that rule.

"How's it feeling?" I asked, pointing at his shoulder. Thankfully, it had only been a sprain the other night and not a full separation.

"Good as new." Axel grinned. "You saw my unit score, right?" He grinned from ear to ear.

I laughed and dragged my bag to the truck. "You emailed it to me three times."

He hunched like he was celebrating a goal and mouthed, "Eighty-seven percent!" then cupped his hands around his mouth and made the sound of a crowd roaring.

I reached out and cupped his face, pouting my lips. "I'm so proud of you, little guy."

He snorted, then reached for my bag and put it in the truck.

Shar ran down the steps with a pillow tucked under one arm and a tote bag full of snacks. "Let's go!"

We piled into the truck, Axel between me and Crystal in the back, and the doors slammed in chorus. The city fell away quickly, replaced by long stretches of highway and mountains that grew with every mile. We stopped for gas somewhere outside Canmore, piling out to stretch and complain about Axel insisting on sitting with his legs at forty-five degree angles, crushing us against the windows.

"My boys need to breathe!" He said, then bought a bag of red licorice and made us answer stupid "Would you rather?" questions before he'd share.

It took another hour before we reached the turnoff. Axel

leaned forward. "Okay, we're looking for a sign with a hand-painted falcon on it . . . yep! That's it." He pointed excitedly.

"Have you been here before?" Crystal asked.

"When I was a kid." Axel directed Rob up the dirt road. We bumped along for what felt like forever until suddenly the woods opened up and there it was. A two-story log house with faded teal shutters, wide wooden steps, and a porch swing. Moss crept along the edges of the stone chimney, and the lawn had a dozen planters overflowing with wildflowers even though it was barely spring.

Shar let out a low whistle. "Wow. You weren't kidding. It's gorgeous."

"I told you. My Great Aunt Sylvia knows what she's doing, eh. This place didn't have indoor plumbing when she bought it." He hopped out of the truck after Rob parked. "Now we've got heat, running water, and a hot tub out back."

Axel and Rob unloaded our bags, and we carried them up to the porch. It was still mud season up here, and the driveway was a bit of a mess.

"You have the key?" Rob asked.

"Do I have the key?" Axel scoffed and reached under a rock next to the porch. He pulled out a rusted metal box. Inside there was a key with a heart-shaped top and a little hand-written tag: *Welcome home, kiddo.*

He smiled at it before unlocking the door and swinging it open with a theatrical flourish.

The inside was even better than the outside, if that was possible. High ceilings with exposed beams, mismatched furniture that somehow worked perfectly together, and a fireplace made of river stones. A stack of board games sat in the corner.

"I'm calling dibs on a room." Rob grabbed Shar and dragged her laughing down the hall.

Axel flopped onto the biggest couch with a groan of satisfaction. "I'll take whatever bed, but I'm claiming this spot for the rest of the trip. You can fight me, but I will win."

By early evening, the rest of the crew had arrived. Tim and Nick showed up with Emily in the back, then Rory pulled in with Kelsey. Bear sat crammed in the backseat next to a guitar case.

Everyone tumbled through the door at once, carrying duffels, mini hockey sticks, and enough food to feed a small army. After determining bedrooms by a rock-paper-scissors competition, we all ended up back in the main room off the kitchen.

Crystal and I ended up in the cozy upstairs room with the slanted ceiling and the antique floral wallpaper. Shar and Rob claimed the main floor master and won the challenge brought by Bear and Kelsey. Rory and Axel ended up in what we quickly dubbed "the bunkhouse," a room with two twin beds, mismatched blankets, and walls covered in crocheted woodland animals. The other couples took the bedrooms in the basement.

Now the guys were playing mini hockey in the living room. Shar had wisely moved all the lamps.

"Your goal is too narrow." Bear pointed at a dining room chair, and Nick nudged it out a bit.

"Fine, happy?"

"Still a little to the right." Bear grinned, and Nick flipped him the bird.

I followed Crystal into the office where Rob was geeking out over the computer. "This is better than what they have at Douglas."

I marveled at the beast of a desktop with a CD-ROM drive and a monitor the size of a microwave. There was even a printer, complete with a stack of fresh dot matrix paper. It made me want to do homework. Which was a thought I kept inside my body.

I was grateful for the distractions because anytime my brain had downtime, I circled back to Chase. What was he doing this weekend? Was he pissed that I still had his sweatshirt? Was he thinking about me at all?

We ended the night with frozen pizza, hot chocolate, and way too many bodies crammed into the backyard hot tub under the stars. Someone brought out a boombox, and Axel gave us a striptease to Bryan Adams. We truly didn't need alcohol to act like idiots. It was probably my favourite thing about us.

———

We woke early the next morning for a hike—Axel's idea, fueled by a map he found in the drawer next to the Trivial Pursuit boardgame. The trails were half-frozen and half-slush, and my boots were soaked through in minutes. But the views?

Breathtaking.

Towering pines gave way to sweeping vistas of the Rocky Mountains, their jagged peaks dusted in late snow, lit gold by the rising sun. A frozen lake shimmered below, the surface fractured like stained glass. Birds cut through the air, and we crossed over not one, but two waterfalls churning with snowmelt.

By the time we got back to the cabin, our legs were aching and our socks were soggy, but our spirits had never been higher. After showering and putting on loungewear, I showed up in the living room to find nobody there.

Voices wafted from the office, so I followed my ears and found nearly the entire group huddled around the computer. I wormed my way into the mass. "What's going on?"

Sharla yanked me closer, pointing at the screen. "Rob got an email. From the scout that held that exhibition."

My eyes flared. I leaned over the chair, squinting at the text on the screen.

"Okay, okay." Rob waved his hand to quiet us. "Here's what it says." The room stilled. He cleared his throat. "'Rob, great to see you on the ice last week. Your speed and composure caught our attention.'" He grinned. "Obviously," he added, then continued on, summarizing. "They're assembling a development squad for a three-month travel intensive. Starts June first. Fifteen players. Three coaches. Two scouts. Exhibition games across Quebec and Ontario with NHL feeder team staff in attendance.'"

Crystal let out a low whistle. "Holy. Shit."

"Keep going." Tim rocked his chair.

Rob scrolled. "Accommodation, gear, and travel provided. Training will be full-time. No part-time schooling or employment permitted."

"Does it roll into next semester?" Axel asked.

"If it starts in June, yeah. It would, eh?" Rory mused.

"Coach Wilson was telling us some of those scouts work with the Mooseheads, bud," Nick said.

"Mooseheads, IceDogs, even the Marlies," Rory added. "I know two guys who went through that dev squad and got signed to the AHL."

The weight of it hit all at once. Shar pursed her lips. "This is incredible, babe."

Rob turned, searching her face. "I'd be away for a bit."

She blinked quickly and smiled. "Hell yes, you will."

Rob stood from the chair and hugged her. Rory and Bear joined in, slamming them against the wall.

"Shit! Careful with my Auntie's house, boys!" Axel laughed and yanked them away from anything breakable. Rob made the rounds, getting hugs and slapping backs.

That's when I noticed her. Shar. Escaping through the doorway into the hall.

I gave it a minute—just long enough for the chaos to spike again—then slipped out after her and wound my way to her bedroom past the kitchen.

The door was cracked. I knocked softly, waited a moment, then pushed it open.

Shar sat on the bed, legs curled beneath her, facing the window. One hand was pressed over her mouth. Her shoulders shook.

"Shar?" I rushed to her, sitting on the bed and wrapping my arm around her shoulders.

She didn't turn. Didn't speak. Just reached to her side and held something out without looking. It took a second for my eyes to focus, but when my brain processed what I was looking at, I gasped.

A pregnancy test. With two pink lines staring up at me.

CRYSTAL, Shar, and I tucked ourselves into our upstairs bedroom while the boys celebrated below us. Crystal shut the door and flipped the lock as Shar settled on my bed cross-legged and snatched a pillow to hug. Her face was blotchy, her eyes red-rimmed, but her breathing had settled.

Crystal perched beside her and I sat at the edge of the bed. "So . . . your due date would be when?"

Sharla sniffed. "Probably November sometime? I don't remember exactly when my last period ended."

I counted out the months from June. Rob would be back in September, so that was good.

Shar twisted the corner of the pillow between her fingers. "I was going to tell Rob when we got back. I had this plan. I knew I was late. I took a test before we left and the line was super faint, but I still bought this little Douglas baby hat and was going to give it to him after I checked again but—" Her voice cracked.

Crystal leaned her head on Shar's shoulder. "Nothing has changed, babe."

Shar shook her head. "It has. You saw his face. He has this opportunity—once in a lifetime. And even though it's only three months, if he does well, there will be more—"

"But you can go with him," I countered.

"Not unless I want to drop out of school! And with a baby?" Her eyes filled again, but she blinked fast, pressing her fingers against her temple. "He won't be able to focus. I can't take that from him."

I blew out a breath. She had a point. "Okay. Let's game this out. Look at the options."

Crystal nodded. "Yes, please."

I chewed my lower lip, thinking. "Option one—the obvious one—you keep the baby, and Rob still goes. You stay in school. You figure it out here."

Shar's jaw tightened. "Alone."

"Not alone," I said firmly. "You have us. Rob's family." I wasn't going to mention hers since she hadn't fully ironed things out with them yet, and I didn't blame her. "You'd have support. But it would be hard."

She nodded slowly, not arguing.

"Option two," I continued, "you have the baby, but you go with him. You take a semester off. Maybe defer some classes. You'd be there for the start of everything with him."

Shar's eyes flicked to the wall, considering.

"But that changes your path," Crystal added gently. "Graduation and everything. It puts that on hold."

Shar blew out a breath. "And we'd probably have to pay for our own housing. I'd be pregnant in a new place, trying to figure out healthcare in another province."

I nodded. "Yeah. So then there's option three. You don't keep the baby. There's adoption or . . . "

The room fell silent.

Shar blinked hard, looking down at her lap. "No. Neither of those are options."

I exhaled slowly. I wasn't going to judge her in the least for considering them. "Okay. Then I think you have to tell Rob."

Shar's lip trembled. "Rob wants to be a dad." She leaned back against the headboard, staring at the ceiling. I gave her a minute. "I don't want to tell him yet. I want him to just be happy. He's worked so hard . . . "

Crystal rubbed her knee. "Then don't. Tell him when you want to."

I opened my mouth to agree with her when the door handle jiggled. All three of us jumped.

"Hey, Mads? Is Shar in there?"

Rob's voice. Crystal and I stared at Sharla.

"Yep! Just chatting." Shar tried to make her voice sound cheery and mostly succeeded.

There was a pause. Then Rob said, "You okay?"

Shar teared up again, and another knock sounded. "Mads, open the door."

I gave Shar a questioning look. Tears welled in her eyes, and she motioned for me to open it. "You sure?" I whispered. Shar nodded.

"Mads—"

"I'm coming, geez." I dropped off the bed and walked to the door. As soon as I flicked the lock, Rob turned the handle and stormed in. He scanned the room fast. Sharla. Crystal. Me. The tissue box. The puffy faces.

His jaw tightened. "What the hell is going on?" He rushed forward, dropping to his knees at the side of the bed. "Is this about the offer? I can—"

"No." Sharla swiped at her cheeks, then turned to him. "I'm so proud of you, Rob. I can't even—" She pursed her lips, sucking in a shaky breath. "I didn't want to tell you today. I didn't want to make this day about anything else."

"Tell me what?" Rob searched her eyes.

She pulled the test from her pocket and handed it to him. "I'm pregnant."

For a long moment, he didn't move. Didn't blink. Then his hand lifted, cupping her jaw. "You're . . . ?"

"I'm so sorry. This messes up everything—" she started, but Rob held a finger to her lips.

"You will not apologize right now." His voice was raw, his breath stilted. "Holy shit," he murmured, then stood and scooped her off the bed. "I'm going to be a dad?" He wrapped her in his arms. "I'm going to be a dad?" he repeated into her hair.

I stepped back, tears welling in my eyes. I felt like I was intruding on something sacred, but I couldn't look away.

Rob pulled back, planting kisses over Sharla's forehead, her cheeks, murmuring "I love you," over and over again, then raised his voice and yelled, "Boys, get your asses up here now! I'm going to be a frigging dad!"

———

By the time I pulled into my apartment complex, it felt like Friday night had happened in another lifetime. After much discussion over the weekend and with Shar's insistence, Rob had made his decision. He was going with the travel team. The opportunity was too rare to turn down, and they were sure they could figure out the logistics.

I was emotionally spent when I stepped out of the truck and took my bag from Axel, setting it on the curb. I gave a small wave and walked up to the familiar brick of the building but paused at the walkway. My Rabbit was parked in its usual spot beneath the half-dead maple tree, but something green fluttered against the windshield.

I frowned, left my bag next to the grass and crossed the street. A Post-It note clung to the glass, stuck under the wiper on the driver's side.

I plucked it free and found two words. *Miss You.*

I blinked and read them again. My eyes scanned the car, heart already speeding.

The first thing I noticed was the wipers. They were aligned. Snug against the windshield. Then I noticed another flash of green on the passenger seat and yanked open the door. What the hell?

Resting on the seat was a swirl of black plastic, and there was a piece of tape on one end with a handwritten note that said, *Old and very cracked vacuum hoses. Dangerous.* I laughed out loud, thinking of Chase digging under the hood after our first committee meeting.

I picked up the second Post-It. *Please lock your car.*

I pressed the back of my hand to my mouth to smother the laugh threatening to escape. My cheeks burned from the grin that spread like wildfire across my face as I scanned the street, wondering if he was still there, watching.

Chase. I missed him so much it hurt. I couldn't wait to see him at our study sessions and at the same time had been dreading it. Because we still hadn't solved anything. I was still chasing a future across the ocean, he was still not on the market for a student like me, and he still didn't know where he was going next.

Still.

I grinned and grabbed the hoses and his notes, then pressed down the locks on the door, and ran back to the sidewalk.

Somehow I survived until Tuesday afternoon. My heart was nearing palpitations as I crossed campus to the North Centre. I walked in early, praying that I'd find Chase alone and could talk with him for a second before anyone showed up.

But as I swung the door open, every hopeful thought slipped through my fingers like water.

Lamont stood at the chalkboard, his hands on his hips.

He smiled approvingly. "Maddie. Prompt. I like that."

I blinked. "I . . . didn't know you were attending today."

Lamont strode toward a table at the end of the row. "Last minute change, I'm afraid. I'll be here the rest of the semester."

The air seemed to thin. "Oh, really? Why is that?"

"Coach Kaplan's wife was in a serious accident last week. Broadsided downtown. He's taking an indefinite leave to care for her."

My heart lurched. "That's terrible. Is she okay?"

"She'll recover, but it's going to be an uphill road. She'll need full-time help. Coach Wilson stepped in as assistant coach. Just confirmed it yesterday. Which means I'm stepping in for him."

I nodded, too stunned to speak.

Lamont patted the chair next to him. "Please. Fill me in."

THE WEEKS after our cabin getaway passed in a blur. Equal parts adrenaline and caffeine to get me through my cramming for midterms after working with the Outlaws.

That first Tuesday with Lamont, the study session was at capacity, and it didn't let up. The team was invested, and I could barely get to everything in the two hours allotted.

I thought up new lesson ideas when I knew I hadn't gotten a concept across, then bolted to the library to get my own hours in. To make matters worse, my mind didn't love focusing on anything that wasn't Chase related. I couldn't tell if not seeing him or sneaking glimpses of him during practice after our study sessions was worse. Those moments dangled him in front of me when I couldn't do anything about it.

I missed him so much it physically ached. Which was why when I saw Chase's name in my inbox the Thursday before Nationals, I almost choked on my own spit.

Hey,

Would love to go over the numbers ahead of the weekend. You free tomorrow?

—C

I read it twice, my throat tightening. Numbers? I hadn't talked with him in a couple of weeks, and he wanted to talk numbers?

Fine. I would talk numbers. I forgot all about why I'd decided not to reach out to Chase in the first place, why it didn't make sense to pursue this, and started typing.

Sure. I'll come to your office before the study session.
—M

I logged out of the computer and grabbed my bag, the line "What would Crystal do?" running through my head.

Time to pick out a good, tight tank top. Because I was showing up braless.

———

My confidence had waned by at least sixty percent by the time I stood in front of Chase's office. I straightened my shirt, then opened the door and walked in. His secretary wasn't there, so I rounded the desk and found Chase's door wide open.

"Hey." He stood from his chair, still analyzing something on the paper in front of him. He finally set it down and looked up.

His eyes settled below my neck, flared, then flicked up to my face. I stifled a grin. That was so worth it.

"Hey." I set my bag next to the chair. "Worried about Nationals?"

Chase's jaw hung slack. "Uh . . . You look—I mean, sorry, I haven't seen you in a minute and . . . " He lifted his eyes, his throat working. "I'm having trouble not staring at your chest."

I pressed my lips together. *Damn it.* Why was he so . . . Chase? "I'm sorry." I looked down at my nipples clearly visible through the fabric. "I was mad."

His brows pulled together. "At me?"

"Yes, at you." I put my hands on my hips, then thought better of it and crossed my arms over my chest. "You emailed me like I was just a—" I shook my head. "A colleague."

Chase tapped his fingers on the desk. "But you left my room in Clearwater. You said—"

"I know what I said."

Chase cocked his head to the side, then rounded his desk and walked to the door. He flicked the lock, then reached for the string at the edge of the blinds hanging over the glass and closed them.

When he turned to face me, his chest was heaving. "I was trying not to be obvious."

I sucked in a breath, taking in his dilated pupils, the slight part of his lips. "You don't want to talk about numbers?"

Chase shook his head. "No. I don't want to talk about numbers." He closed the distance between us in two strides, then pulled me against him, his lips crashing into mine.

Hell, yes. Every cell in my body lit up like a Christmas tree. Chase ran his hands over my back, over my butt, then pulled me with him back to his chair. He sat, dragging me into his lap. His hands gripped my hips as he kissed me, like he couldn't decide if he wanted to pull me closer or hold me still. I shifted forward, my thighs tightening against his as my hair fell on either side of his face.

I'd missed this. Missed *him.* The taste of his mouth. The smell of his skin. The way he made everything else in the world go blessedly quiet.

"Thank you. For fixing my car," I rasped between kisses. I tugged at his lips with my teeth, working to unbutton his shirt.

"No problem." He slid his hands under my shirt, hissing through his teeth when he didn't meet any resistance moving north.

"We were stupid," I murmured, kissing his jaw, nipping at his neck. My head swirled, everything we'd talked about jumbling into a chaotic mess. Chase wasn't my professor, and who cared what my mom thought? If she wanted to judge me, she could judge me, but nobody here besides Shar and Crystal knew that Chase was once my stepbrother. And yes, it would royally suck if and when I left in the fall, but if Chase stayed—if he took Kaplan's job for next year—we'd have all summer and probably fall semester even if I did get the scholarship. And that was a big if.

Chase grunted as I finally got his shirt open and ran my hands over his bare chest.

"It's stupid to not be together when I don't even know if I'm going anywhere." I threw my head back as Chase moved his lips to my neck, crushing me against him, rolling my hips.

"You're going to go." His voice rumbled in my chest.

"Not great odds and—" I whimpered as he slipped the strap of my tank top over my shoulder and kissed lower. This was what I needed. I couldn't think past the feel of his hands, the heat of his breath. Couldn't worry about midterms or summer work or extending my lease or—

"You'll get it." He pushed my hair to the side, kissing his way back to my jaw.

"Maybe I don't even want it anymore."

As soon as the words left my lips, Chase stilled. He pulled back and looked up at me, his lips swollen, his eyes dark. "Don't say that."

I worked to catch my breath. "I was just thinking—"

"I know what you were thinking." Chase slid me back on his thighs. He replaced my tank top strap and rested his hands on my hips, then closed his eyes and drew a deep breath. "I'm sorry." He exhaled in a rush.

"Sorry about what?" My pulse raced, a pit opening up in my stomach. "Chase—"

"This is selfish of me." He tapped my thigh and gently lifted me off him. When I stood, he adjusted himself and took a minute to breathe before standing. "You need to focus on your scholarship, and I—"

"What?" I straightened my shirt, my eyes stinging. "Don't tell me what I need to focus on."

"Don't change your plans because of me." He ran a hand through his hair. "I don't know where I'm going to be—"

"But we both have choices. We can decide—"

"You've already decided."

"Partially."

He raised an eyebrow. "You asked to tutor because you wanted this scholarship more than anything."

"Not all of us only want one thing," I snapped, and instantly regretted it. The sadness returned to Chase's eyes, but anger welled in me so thick, I couldn't soften enough to take it back.

Why was he being like this? For all his talk about not wanting, about letting things be what they were going to be, he was the one who emailed me. He obviously wanted something from this.

Chase dropped his eyes. "Well. I want you to get the Rhodes."

I wet my lips. "And what about for you?"

His jaw tensed and released. "I need to work on some things for Nationals. I'm sorry—"

I picked up my bag and stormed out of his office before he could finish that sentence.

CHAPTER
Twenty~Four

WE ENTERED the commons area of the North Centre and the rich, buttery scent of popcorn hit me first. Someone had dragged in a popcorn machine from the theatre department and set it next to a massive drink cooler labeled "Outlaws Fuel" in red marker. Two hours before puck drop, the place was already half full.

Shar, Crystal, and I had spit-balled a thousand ways to be in person for the Outlaws games at Nationals, but when Douglas announced they'd be playing them on the big screen, we decided to stay put with the rest of the student body.

In the middle of the tables, a mammoth projector unit faced a makeshift screen mounted to the far wall. Someone had hung fleece Outlaws blankets over the windows to darken the space. Brilliant.

"I'm so nervous, my hands are shaking." Crystal clenched her fists as we claimed our spot at the front-left table. She dropped her bag with a thunk and immediately pulled out her scarf. "I want more hockey tournaments."

"Just so you can skip class?" Shar asked.

I grinned. "It's not skipping when the professor okays it."

Kowalski let us out early as long as we promised to do an extra problem set and turn them in over the weekend in his drop box.

Shar eased into her seat beside us, tugging her coat off and exposing her barely there baby bump. "I got a full extension on my term paper. I told them I was emotionally compromised. Technically true."

We waited while one of the more techie staffers at Douglas got the feed going, then focused on the warm-ups. Our bracket was steep. It was double elimination, but we had to win our way through the gauntlet. The Outlaws had drawn one of the strongest BC teams in the first round. Okanagan's Silverhawks. I was already regretting leaving Chase's office instead of actually looking at the data he had.

The room erupted at puck drop. We only left our seats between periods to use the washroom and grab snacks, and when the final buzzer sounded, there were hugs and congrats all around. Final score: Douglas 3–1.

Game two against the Langley Northstars was tighter. They pressed harder. Rob went bar-down in OT, and the screen flickered just enough that for one heart-stopping second, we weren't sure if it had gone in.

We were hoarse by game three. The Outlaws took on Red River College, and the game was a grinder from start to finish. No clean plays, no flow. Just grit and persistence. Somehow they pulled out 4-2 by the end of the second. But in the third, Red River scored in the first three minutes, then again on a power play with three minutes left. Blakely pulled Tim at two minutes in a go-for-the-glory move, but it didn't pay off. An empty netter from one of the Red River forwards sealed our fate.

The mood on campus was somber until we realized they were still playing for third.

Somehow we managed to turn in our homework and take care of basic living while spending four-plus hours in the North Centre every day. When we showed up for the bronze medal match, we found familiar faces on the big screen.

"Shut up! Interviews!" someone shouted, and we tuned in to Blakely talking about the Douglas offense. I was about to hit the washroom before puck drop when Chase's face filled the screen. My stomach flipped.

"I know that loss in the semis probably still stings. I'm sure you've been making some adjustments," the reporter said. "What do you think will be the difference tonight?"

Chase nodded. "Yeah, honestly? I'm not upset about that loss. We played good hockey, and the puck happened to bounce in their favour a few times, but we're going to stick with our game and play steady tonight."

"And what is it that defines your game?"

Chase considered a moment, then answered, "If you'd asked me that before the holidays, I probably would've given a different answer, but now I'd say it's preparation. Discipline. Paying attention to the numbers." Chase looked up, straight into the camera. "We've been lucky enough to have some fantastic training, someone helping us work on analytics. It's helped us put our guys in the best position to use their strengths."

Crystal grabbed my arm. I couldn't breathe. Chase hadn't said my name, but he'd just given me a shout out on national TV. The interviewer thanked him, and Chase shook his hand, then looked up again and—

"He winked!" Shar pointed at the screen. "Did you see that?" She whirled in her seat, grinning. "Maddie—"

"I saw it." I gave her a look, willing her not to draw any more attention.

I escaped to the washroom, his words replaying in my head. What the hell did Chase Wilson want? He wanted me, but then wouldn't let me make choices to want him back? He wanted to coach, but then wouldn't say out loud what type of position he was looking for? He wouldn't make plans or admit that there was anything worth trying for, and while I understood where that came from, I didn't like it.

I plopped down next to Crystal and Shar, hoping I could

forget for the next few hours and just get lost in the game. But I knew I'd be disappointed. Because Chase's touch was the only thing that allowed me to be fully present.

The Outlaws came out against Manitoba Tech like they had something to prove. Chase and Blakely worked the bench like a chessboard. They rotated lines with precision. The guys played loose, fast, and electric. It was 3-1 before the second period even started.

Manitoba rallied in the beginning of the third, but Douglas held them 3-2 until the buzzer sounded.

Douglas had medaled. *At Nationals.*

People in the North Centre screamed, hugged, and cried. Sharla, Crystal, and I stared at the screen in awe. It was the first time that Douglas had ever placed, and it was our boys who did it.

———

Three days later, the crowd outside the Douglas Dome pulsed with cheers and whistles, the tinny bray of the student pep band squawking out a peppy version of "We Are the Champions." I stood shoulder to shoulder with Crystal and Sharla near the edge of the crowd, wrapped in our maroon-and-gold scarves.

"Isn't there another victory song we could pull into the mix?" Crystal muttered as the chorus kicked in for the third time.

"It's Queen. It never gets old," I teased.

Sharla was quiet, her hands tucked over her belly.

"Nervous?" I asked.

She sighed. "Just thinking."

"About what?" Crystal undid the buttons of her jacket. It was getting warm in the sun.

"All of this. Rob. Hockey." She grazed her teeth over her

lower lip. "I don't think he can be happy without this. And I know that if he played pro he'd find a team and we could be more settled, but . . . "

I let out a breath. "If he doesn't."

She nodded. "Right. If he doesn't."

My conversation with Chase flickered in my head. *This is their backup plan.* My thoughts moved from Rob to the rest of the guys on the team. The ones who hadn't been invited to join the summer travel team. One year left, and then what? Beer leagues?

A shout rippled through the crowd as the players filed onto the makeshift stage set up in front of the Dome. Cheers swelled as Bear waved his arms to pump everyone up. Axel blew a kiss to a group of freshmen at the front.

"They're so much more creative than we were," Crystal noted, staring at signs that read "Bear Down" and "#47 is my Daddy" in glitter glue.

Blakely stood behind them, arms folded, squinting into the sun. I waited, watching for Chase, but when Blakely stepped up to the mic and launched into a speech, he still wasn't there.

"First-ever Nationals medal for Douglas. I'd like to say I always believed we'd get here, but the truth is, these boys surprised the hell outta me."

Laughter. Cheers. He clapped a hand on Rob's shoulder and continued, but I wasn't listening. He wasn't there. Why wasn't he there?

"If I could take just a minute."

My head snapped up at the sound of Rob's voice. Sharla straightened next to me.

"This has been the best season of my life. Not just because we won bronze. But because of what this team's become. A family." He looked down at the crowd, searching until his eyes landed on us. His smile widened. "I got offered a spot on a development team," he said to cheers and whoops. "Everyone says it could be a foot in the door. Said it could lead to something big."

The cheers continued, but he held up a hand and the noise faltered.

"I was all in, ready to pack up and leave at the end of May, but something happened while we were gone at Nationals. I realized that I didn't care about the door anymore. Or what was behind it. Not if it meant missing out on the family I found. The family I'm building."

The crowd cheered at that, and Rob raised his voice. "I'll be staying here at Douglas because there's someone outside of these guys behind me who stands by me every step of the way. She's the most important person in my life, and Sharla, if you'll get up here, I have a question for you." Rob dropped to one knee as the crowd exploded.

Sharla stood shaking next to me. "He's not joining the team?"

I laughed, tears stinging my eyes. "Doesn't look like it."

"But—"

I gave her a little nudge, and that was all she needed. The crowd cheered as she walked to the stairs, then quieted when she ascended to stand in front of Rob. He pulled something from his pocket, and Axel grabbed the mic, holding it to his mouth.

"You hate being in front of people," Sharla whispered, the mic barely picking her up.

"Unless he's on skates!" someone shouted, and they both laughed.

"Yeah, well, I needed you to know that I'm serious." Rob lifted his hand, holding up something that glinted gold. "Sharla, I love you." His voice broke as he reached for her hand.

"I'm going to pass out," Crystal hissed next to me, and I wrapped my arm around her. I was also currently struggling to breathe.

"Will you marry me?" Rob asked.

Sharla didn't hesitate. She yelled a "Yes!" then shoved the ring on her finger and yanked him up to kiss her. Axel whooped, then pulled out a tiny, red Outlaws onesie. Crystal and I *awww'd* in unison. I'd ogled the baby stuff in the bookstore on more than one occasion, and I couldn't handle it when he turned it around. On the back, stitched in gold letters, was the number twenty-three. "Like dad!" Axel crowed, and the crowd went bonkers.

Crystal wrapped her arm around my waist. "Is there any part of you that worries?"

I nodded. "You know me." Every part of me worried for them. Shar was going to have a baby, and even though they lived under the same roof, they'd only been *together* together for a few months.

I sighed. "But if anyone could make it . . . "

"Yeah. I know. It's them." Crystal swiped at her eyes. "I shouldn't have worn mascara."

I laughed, pulling her toward the stage. *Our friends were getting married. Our friends were having a baby.* Awe, elation, gratitude, fear, grief, and a thousand other emotions swirled inside me as we approached the stage. Blakely and a handful of other Douglas administrators, including Lamont, congratulated our players.

We squealed and celebrated with Shar, inspected the ring Rob had chosen—a thin gold band with beveled edges—promising to come over later. Crystal moved over to talk with Rory, and with everyone momentarily occupied, I slipped between Tim and Bear to snag Axel. "Hey, where's Coach Wilson?"

Axel frowned. "Why?"

"Just—" I pursed my lips. "Do you know or not?"

Axel's eyes narrowed. "He had to go home. Said it was a family thing."

My throat thickened, all of my suspicions ringing true. *A family thing.* "When you called him, when I didn't answer the day I was supposed to show up at your meeting, how did you get his number?"

Axel shrugged. "I just got it from Coach Kaplan's office. They keep a file. He's got a personal info sheet in his file folder."

Of course he did. But Kaplan's office was now Chase's, and if he wasn't there— "Thank you." I gave him a quick hug. "Congrats!"

"Maddie—"

I rushed off, feeling only a little guilty for ditching him mid-sentence, and headed straight for Blakely.

"Coach!" I snagged him before he turned to the stairs. "Do you happen to have Chas— Coach Wilson's address?" His brow furrowed, and I quickly added, "I wanted to take over some cookies. To thank him for letting me work with the team this semester and to say congratulations." I gave my most innocent smile. *No we were not making out in his office with the door locked less than a week ago.*

Blakely eyed me for a long beat. Then he nodded slowly. "Sure. I'll jot it down." He pulled his folder from the microphone stand and flipped it open, then pulled a pen from his jacket pocket. I tapped my foot impatiently. When he handed me the paper, I blinked. Two addresses. His and Chase's.

I flashed a smile. "You'll get the first dozen." Then I turned and bolted from the stage.

CHAPTER
Twenty-Five

THE ENGINE STUTTERED on the first try. I gripped the wheel and turned the key again, coaxing the Rabbit into a reluctant cough, then exhaled as it groaned to life. It was going to die at some point, but today was not that day.

I threw it into reverse, fishtailing slightly on the gravel lot behind the North Centre before hopping onto the main road. I didn't know if Chase would be at his house, and I had no idea if showing up there was going to help or make things worse. But I couldn't go home knowing that he was potentially dealing with his mom getting out of prison on his own.

Rain spit on my windshield, and my wipers cleared a perfect, streak free path over the glass. That only made the ache in my chest sink deeper. Blakely had given me general directions, and I only had to consult my pocket map of Calgary once before I finally turned onto his street. His place was at the end—small, older, one story with stucco siding. It looked clean and neat with a newly painted door.

The shades were drawn. I parked anyway, then climbed the steps and knocked.

Waited.

Knocked again.

Nothing. No sounds inside, only the chirped alarm from a Bluejay who must've had a nest nearby to make that much racket.

I sank down onto the front step, knees drawn up to my chest, the concrete cool through my jeans, and started the glorious pattern of second-guessing myself. I hadn't talked with Chase since that incredibly hot but abbreviated makeout session in his office. He'd pushed me away, so why would I think he'd want me here?

This connection I felt—this pull. It was crazy, wasn't it? How well did I know him, really? Nothing about our relationship, if you could call it that, followed the patterns everyone else talked about. We'd never dipped our toes in the pool. It was either me standing on the deck watching or both of us diving into the deep end. We knew too much and too little about each other—the real things and hardly any of the surface level.

I scraped my shoes against the sidewalk. What if . . . What if he'd already left. For good. That thought slammed into me like a ton of bricks.

The season was over, wasn't it? But would he have left so soon after getting back? Without saying goodbye? Maybe he'd packed up his things, taken another job, and left the second they got home from the airport. Maybe he didn't want to be here when his mom got out, maybe—

The lock clicked behind me. I straightened and turned.

The door opened and there he was.

Grey sweatpants. Bare chest. Eyes bloodshot and hair mussed like he hadn't slept in days. My heart cracked open and rushed to fill the space between us.

I stood up too fast, nearly tripped over my own feet, and every "what if" or "maybe" drained out of me as I wrapped my arms around him.

There were no words. Just a whoosh of air as his hand curled around the back of my head and we breathed into each other.

Chase curled around me, pulling me inside and closing the

door. He dragged me past the half wall in his entry and dropped to the couch, spreading me over him as he lay back on the pillows. His legs nestled between mine, and my heart stumbled a few times before syncing with his rhythm.

I rested my head on his shoulder, closing my eyes as he played with my hair. I had no concept of time. It could've been ten minutes or an hour before he murmured, "I was there. This morning when she got out."

I nodded, my cheek still pressed against his collarbone. I didn't want to say anything to break the flow of his thoughts.

His chest expanded under me. "It wasn't awful. Wasn't great." He let out a slow breath. "She looked older. Tired. She cried when she saw me. Probably didn't think I'd show up."

I lifted my hand to his cheek, sliding my fingers until they were on either side of his ear, then brushed my thumb over his jaw. Here he was telling me one of the hardest things I could imagine, and there was no tangled mess behind my ribs. No pressure in my head. His body was like a plug-in outlet when I'd been living solely on battery power.

"She's staying at a halfway house near Brentwood," Chase continued. "They've got a good program. I'll check in on her. Help her get on her feet."

I pondered the right words to say, and when I couldn't find them, went with, "You're a good son." It's what I would want to hear from my dad if he were here. That I'd made him proud. That I was everything he'd hoped I'd be.

Chase was quiet. I just curled my fingers into his side and held him. Eventually, he shifted me to the side so he could look at me. "I got an offer."

I searched his eyes, trying to discover his news before he said it, searching for excitement or sadness—anything to give me a clue.

"An assistant coaching position. In Vancouver."

My lungs stuttered. That was so far away. "From who?" I worked to keep the panic out of my voice.

"Capilano. It's not high profile, but they've got a good program. Decent funding. I'd get to help rebuild it from the ground up."

Capilano. Vancouver. The image of Blakely standing outside Chase's hotel room in Clearwater flared in my mind like a match. *There's a player who wants to talk to you . . .*

Had he known that night? Or at least had an idea?

"Are you going to take it?" I asked.

Chase dropped his gaze. "It would be smart."

I wanted to ask about Douglas, about potential opportunities here, but I couldn't do it. He was here because of a connection through his dad. He was a compliance coach, even if he was currently filling in for Kaplan.

He said he didn't want, but we both knew this wasn't even close to his end game.

"I don't want you to leave," I whispered, my eyes already stinging. This wasn't about me. He'd been with his mom at a prison this morning, and I didn't want to add more of a burden, but I couldn't keep the words from spilling out.

Chase pushed my curls back from my face. "I thought you were leaving first." The corner of his mouth lifted, and I coughed a laugh.

"I wanted to leave first. I didn't actually do it."

Chase grinned, and everything I wanted to say jumbled in my head.

"You're thinking too hard." He pressed a kiss to my forehead, then pulled me against his chest. I didn't respond because I didn't want to hear the words I was certain he'd follow with. *Whatever happens, happens. It will be what it's going to be.*

Screw that. I didn't want to float through life and hope I got where I wanted to go. I wanted to fight for it, even if I lost.

But I couldn't fight for this alone. Chase had a job offer. He had a thousand reasons not to want to stay here in Calgary or work at Douglas. So instead of flaying myself open and pouring out my heart, I said, "Write me?"

He chuckled, the sound rumbling through my chest. "Send me cookies?"

I grinned, needling him in the ribs. "Those you only get in person."

It was either both of us diving in the deep end.

Or me, standing on the deck.

THE LAST MONTH of the semester passed in a blur of late-night study sessions, phone calls to landlords when our fridge went out, and too many trips to Tim Hortons. Crystal and I were deep in finals prep, but we managed to find enough time to help Shar and Rob look for a new place. It had two bedrooms and was closer to campus than my place.

I filled every spare second. It helped keep my mind off of Chase, wherever he was at the moment. That is until I crawled into bed at night and then, no matter how tired I was, I couldn't keep thoughts of him out of my head. It was the sweetest torture.

Shar's spring concert rode the heels of moving chaos and landed two days before final exams. The Rozsa Centre was packed, and Shar looked radiant in the black satin dress she still fit into. She was worried about having to buy a new wardrobe, but I, for one, couldn't wait until her belly was big enough to rub.

The moment the final piece ended—a lush, soaring rendition of *Scheherazade*—our group erupted.

"THAT'S OUR GIRL, SHAR!" Axel bellowed, loud enough that an older man in the front row adjusted his hearing aid. Bear whistled through his fingers, and I had to tug on Rob's sleeve to keep him from jumping up on his chair.

I couldn't stop smiling.

We headed to Ranchman's the night finals wrapped up. The team had just gotten their marching orders for the offseason, but for the moment, we were all free as birds. Rob danced with his arm slung over Shar's shoulder, gently rocking her in time with the music. Bear and Nick kept the pitchers of beer replenished, and Rory challenged two girls to a game of pool. Which he lost. Crystal pretended not to know him until he dipped her on the dance floor and whispered something that made her laugh so hard she dropped her clutch.

When the three of us reconvened at our table an hour later, Shar looked tired. Her smile didn't quite reach her eyes as she watched Rob put Nick in a headlock.

"Everything okay?" Crystal asked.

Shar kept her face a mask of calm. "What if he starts to resent me? Or the baby? What if he gives it all up and then hates me for it?"

My heart squeezed. "You saw his speech. He seemed pretty sure of himself."

She scoffed. "Sure, he is now. But what about after the baby comes? What about when we're up all night and still trying to finish our classes? What about when he can't just be like this with the team, and it's his last year, and then—" Her lips drew into a line. "What about in five years? Ten?"

I didn't have an answer.

"Everything has to end eventually, doesn't it?" Crystal mused.

It was true. I'd played soccer in elementary and middle school, but after that the only option was the high school team, which I had no interest in trying out for. Basketball was the same. You either got serious and made the teams or you were done.

I frowned. Why was it like that for youth sports? For adult

sports, especially hockey? If there were over fifty thousand youth hockey players in Canada, why was there only one path for competitive play? Why wasn't anyone building something for all those players living their backup plans?

My brain lit up like it always did when a good puzzle presented itself.

I needed to do more research.

———

After a blustery spring storm, campus felt like the inside of a snow globe that had been shaken and left to settle. It was quiet and draped in thick, wet snow as I took my usual spot in front of the computers in the library.

Finals were over. Half the dorms had emptied. The coffee shop was running on reduced hours, and the only other person in the library looked like he'd fallen asleep over his notes three days ago and no one had the heart to wake him.

I pulled out my stack of legal pads and a pen, then logged in with my student ID. I wasn't sure what I was trying to find, but the question that caught my attention at Ranchman's wouldn't release its claws.

I waited for the internet to dial up, then dug in. I searched hockey leagues, tournaments, and organizations, took notes on the boards and coaches, then refined my searches. I searched through old newspapers and magazines, scanned articles about youth sports infrastructure, university development programs, minor league foundations, alumni-run travel leagues, women's rec leagues, even intramural models at other universities. I bookmarked pages from the CJHL, the CCHL, the BCHL, even obscure ones like the Thunder Bay Junior B Circuit.

It was a mess of scribbled names, numbers, and acronyms, but at least I had some contact information and a place to start.

I flipped to a clean page and started sketching a rough model. How many players aged out of Juniors every year in Alberta? What percentage dropped out of competitive play entirely? How many moved into coaching or development? How many wanted to but couldn't afford to?

Could there be a place for them? Could there be more?

My pen flew over the page. Equations, cost estimates, notes on liability. I made a note about gear sponsorships and volunteer-run rinks. League insurance. Travel costs. Ice time contracts.

I started crunching numbers like I had with Chase, my determination solidifying. There were so many players. How did nothing competitive exist for them? It seemed ludicrous.

When my head started pounding, I realized I'd forgotten to eat lunch. And dinner.

I stretched my arms over my head, then put away the periodicals before logging out and gathering my notes, tucking them into my bag.

I grabbed a ham-and-cheese wrap from the bookstore, then drove the few blocks to Shar's place, wolfing down the food in the car.

She ushered me in, quick to show off their progress. There were still boxes lining the hall, but she had a few pictures up and the kitchen cupboards were stocked.

Shar, in her leggings and an oversized Calgary Philharmonic hoodie, grabbed my hand and dragged me down the hallway to see the future nursery. They'd painted a soft sage green halfway up the walls, and a rocking chair now sat in the corner.

"It's going to be amazing."

She beamed. "We don't know the gender yet, so we figured we'd go with green."

It was all I could do to follow her back into the living room before opening my backpack. Once she was settled on the couch,

I pulled out my notes. "I've been thinking about what you said the other night."

"Which thing?" She raised an eyebrow, and I huffed a laugh.

"Nothing to do with papier-mâché lingerie, so you might be disappointed."

"I definitely will be."

I grinned, setting the legal pads on the coffee table. "I've been crunching numbers. Looking at how many athletes age out every year with nowhere to go. Not to the AHL, not to Europe, not even to rec leagues. Just . . . done."

Shar's expression sobered. "Yeah?"

I hesitated. "What if we started a conversation? Talked with some of the people who already run leagues for under-eighteen athletes. What if we showed them these numbers and asked about the potential for expanding things?"

Shar blinked at me, then slowly grinned. "Do you think they'd talk with us?"

I shrugged. "I don't know. But I can't stop thinking about it."

Shar put a hand on her belly. "That's good enough for me."

We chatted for another hour or so, spitballing ideas for what our cold calls or emails would even look like. When I finally got home at nine thirty, the sky was streaked pink and gold. Damn, I always loved the start of summer.

I walked to the mailboxes at the corner of our street and pulled out my key. Inside I found a small stack of mostly flyers and advertisements, but as I closed the metal door, a white envelope caught my eye.

I re-locked the box and pulled it out from between a tanning bed coupon and a reminder that Stampede tickets were going on sale.

When I saw the handwriting and the name and address in the top corner, I dropped my keys.

CHAPTER
Twenty~Seven

Maddie,

I meant to write to you the week I left, but I couldn't think of anything worthwhile to say. Then I realized I needed to thank you for coming to my house that day. Not sure how you got my address (sound familiar?), but I'm grateful. I didn't know I needed you until I saw you sitting on the front step.

I'm not in Vancouver. Right now I'm in Montana with a couple of guys I used to play Juniors with. We rented a place near Flathead Lake. It's quiet. Still too cold to get out on the water, but we've been catching up. Doing a bit of fishing.

That makes me think of my dad, surprisingly. It was one of the only things he did with me when I was little that didn't make me afraid of him.

Sorry. That was depressing.

Let me make up for it by telling you something I meant to tell you in the study room, but every time I thought to, I couldn't quite bring myself to do it.

You've always scared the hell out of me.

Not in a bad way. But you were always such a hard worker. You'd sacrifice sleep or parties when you had homework. You'd sit at that kitchen counter until the middle of the night if you didn't understand a problem (I know because that's when I usually wandered in).

And watching that made me feel like I'd been skating through half of my life. Like maybe I only ever gave fifty percent. But there you were, giving a hundred and ten without blinking. When I moved up in hockey, that memory lit a fire under me. It made me want to be better.

You asked why I didn't contact you about the tutoring. Well, that's why. I felt threatened. I was watching my players sink and wasn't making any headway with administration. Then you waltzed in telling me my plan sucked (my words, not yours) and there you were showing me up again. It took me a few days to swallow my pride.

Then when you walked into that committee meeting? I felt about two centimetres high.

I'm sorry I didn't email. It was a soft play. Hoping this letter makes up for it.

Chase

P.S. Do you wear the sweatshirt or is it sitting in your room somewhere?

———

Chase,

Sometimes I think you're remembering someone who's not me. It's flattering that you had such a high opinion of me. The truth is, I didn't have many parties to sacrifice, and I struggled with insomnia. So math was kind of an escape. I know, total nerd.

I've never been good at sitting in uncertainty. I like knowing things. Predicting outcomes. Making sense of the information I have access to. You've never made sense, and sometimes that's still a bit maddening. Just when I think I have you figured out, I find out you're volunteering with a youth organization or you're known for being a stickler for grades with the Outlaws (gasp).

I'd like to tell you I didn't think your plan sucked, but you got me there. However, I've been thinking a lot about what you told me. About a university team being a hockey player's plan B and how they might only get these last couple of years.

I'm not sure where I'm going with this, but it's crazy to me that a sport like this, one these players love so much, would just end. I'm so sorry it ended for you. I know there are some things beyond our control, but maybe some things aren't. Maybe we shouldn't let go of the things we love so easily.

Anyway. Weekend thoughts. I hope you're having a blast in Montana. Your letter more than makes up for your momentary lapse in judgement. Just don't do it again.

Maddie

P.S. I would wear it but I don't want it to stop smelling like you.

THE NHL PLAYOFFS became our soundtrack. Somehow, Blakely convinced the admins to play the games in the North Centre like they had during Nationals, which meant Crystal, Shar, and I were there most nights with the guys. Crystal printed the bracket, and we all made dollar bets. We watched the Devils claw through the rounds, and Shar never quite got over the Blizzard being knocked out in round one. When New Jersey took down Detroit in a clean sweep, Bear was the one who took home thirteen dollars.

After spending a week with my mom, I started a summer job in the admissions office—organizing files, scheduling tours, and answering phones. It may have been the position I was getting paid for, but the work I couldn't stop thinking about was my research. Well, that and checking the mailbox for Chase's letters.

We kept writing. I didn't ask where he went after Montana, but when I got a letter postmarked from Vancouver, my heart dropped to my knees. It wasn't a surprise, I knew he was going there eventually, but it still hurt like a punch to the throat.

This wasn't just a summer gig. He was moving. He wouldn't be coming back.

I did what I did best—put my head down and worked. Chase

may have seen it is a strength, but I couldn't help but start to look at it as only a coping mechanism.

As soon as applications opened for the Rhodes, I compiled my documents, completed my essays including a write up of my experiences with supporting student athletes on the committee, and included Lamont and Kowalski as references. After triple checking the information, I sealed the envelope and set it on my desk. I could turn it in right away, but I didn't want to seem desperate. I opted to wait a few days before stamping it and dropping it in the mail.

That week, Tash was on a road trip with friends and Crystal was in Kamloops visiting her grandma, which meant I had nothing better to do than sit in the library. Emails had started rolling in a few days prior, but the responses were less than exciting.

Hi Madelyn,

Thanks for reaching out. Interesting idea, but unfortunately our current league structure focuses on junior and pro-development pipelines. There's not a ton of demand for older athletes, and the logistics just aren't feasible. Best of luck.

—D. Gerber, Operations Director, WHLA

I sighed, clicking on the next. They were all polite, and all dead ends. No one was outright dismissive, but none of the people I'd contacted seemed remotely interested in the data I'd sent.

Hi Maddie,

Appreciate your message. In our experience, most adult players who don't go pro tend to move on from competitive hockey. Too many life changes, not enough time. A league for that age group would be hard to fund, let alone fill. Take care.

—G. Lewis, League Development, Canadian Minor Hockey
Assoc.

"Still haven't figured out how to take a break?"

I startled, spinning to find Professor Kowalski standing a few feet away, a coffee in hand.

"Hey, good morning."

Professor Kowalski stepped closer, peering at the colour-coded sheets on the desk next to me. "I know this isn't homework."

I sighed, leaning back in my chair. "Nope. New project." He raised an eyebrow, and I tried to give him the short version. "I've been researching adult hockey leagues."

He grunted. "Any particular reason?"

How was I supposed to explain that? I turned my sheets toward him and slid them across the desk. "There are thousands of players in Alberta who don't get to play competitively for some reason or another. If they don't make the cut for the pros, or they graduate and leave their university teams, they're done. There aren't any options besides community rec leagues."

"And that's not a good option?" Kowalski thumbed through my notes.

"It's not the same." I stifled a yawn. "I've been emailing everyone I can find who runs a hockey league. Trying to see if there would be an option for a new league structure—something for players who age out of Juniors or college and don't make it to the minors or NHL."

He let go of the papers and stepped back. "Not your normal area of study."

I sighed. "Yeah."

Kowalski sipped his coffee. "Have you gotten any interest?"

I shook my head. "No. Seems like nobody is very compelled by my numbers."

He gave me a knowing smile. "Are you compelled?"

"Yes," I answered without hesitation. It was the truth. It wasn't just about Chase. Or Rob. Or any one player I'd come to care about. It was the numbers. The patterns. The way they kept pulling at me like thread I couldn't stop unraveling.

Thousands of players aging out every year, most of them never stepping onto competitive ice again. The data was right there—league drop-offs, age curves, training plateaus. They weren't just figures on a page. They were lives. Futures. Potential that didn't vanish just because a draft didn't go their way. Maybe no one else cared, but I did.

"Isn't the purpose of our work to do good? To make changes?" I shook my head. "I don't understand why nobody's even willing to try."

He studied me for a moment, then set his coffee cup down. "I was first published when I was a grad student. I had a paper rejected three times. Fourth time, a small analytics journal picked it up. I was studying voting trends in rural municipalities. Pretty dry stuff, but I had a theory no one else thought had legs."

"What was it?"

"That public trust was more strongly tied to community sports funding than infrastructure spending." Kowalski gave a modest shrug. "Took me a while to convince anyone. But when I did, it changed how some of those towns shaped their budgets. Point is—you don't always know what your work will become when you start. Sometimes the world just needs a little time to catch up."

He gestured toward my pile of papers. "If you believe you've got something here, you could try pitching it as an independent research project. For credit."

My eyes widened. "Is that a possibility?"

Kowalski picked up his coffee cup. "Maddie, what do you think you'd be doing at Oxford as a Rhodes Scholar? Running basic problem sets? You'd be choosing an area of study, contributing something new to the field. This isn't so different."

I stared at him. "But this isn't pure math."

"No," he agreed. "It's applied. It's structural. And it's got real-world implications. You're using analytics to solve a problem with socioeconomic fallout. That's academic gold if you frame it correctly."

My mind spun. "So who would I propose this to?"

"Lamont would have to endorse it, but you already have a connection there." Kowalski said. "If the proposal's solid and you've got faculty support from both departments—math and athletics—you could make a strong case."

My heart picked up speed. What would I make a strong case for? The numbers? The idea? "You'd support something like this?"

He gave me a crooked smile. "I don't make a habit of backing bad ideas. And you're not in the habit of having them. You'd need a timeline. Deliverables. A clear objective for the league and measurable outcomes."

"I told you, nobody was interested in expanding their programming or offering a league for this age group. I wouldn't—"

"You have an ice arena here don't you? Seems to sit empty much of the time." Kowalski stepped back, straightening his jacket. "I'd be glad to look over your proposal if you'd like. When it's ready." He gave a small nod, then turned and walked toward the glass doors.

Twenty~Nine

Maddie,

Vancouver is beautiful. I'm staying with my friend Turtle and his wife. (Don't ask how he got that name.) They're expecting their first baby. Kind of wild to talk with him about becoming a dad. Rob was talking about Sharla expecting a baby in the fall, and all I could think was they seem so young. Then I realized I'm barely a couple of years older and felt like a poser. (Watch out. Graduation ages you.)

The idea of having a family has always been a tough one for me. I never thought I'd want kids. Or to get married, even. I know, strange, considering what good examples I had of an excellent relationship.

But our conversations, as they always do, made me think. For a couple of years now, I've wondered what I have to offer the world (besides killer abs. You're welcome). I wish I had a little of your confidence.

Chase

P.S. I think about you opening the door in only a T-shirt at least once a week.

. . .

———

I STARED at my application for the Rhodes still sitting on my nightstand, then looked back at the papers I held in my hands. I signed the application, but these were signed by Lamont.

It had taken me three days to write up a proposal. Once I put pen to paper, the ideas wouldn't stop coming. I took it to Kowalski, we made a few adjustments, and then I presented everything to Lamont before the weekend.

I couldn't quite believe it. He'd accepted my proposal, and I was set to move forward with the help of dedicated university resources in the next month if I wanted to. It was strange. I'd been working toward applying for the Rhodes all year, and yet this idea that I'd stumbled upon had more forward momentum.

I blew out a breath. It was time I had an actual conversation with my mother.

I dialed my mom's number, then stretched the phone cord across the hall and into my room, closing the door.

"Hello?"

"Hi, Mom."

Her voice brightened. "I've been trying to call you."

"I know, I'm sorry I didn't get back to you earlier."

She scoffed. "Maddie, I'm not your insurance company. I don't want to be a burden."

I sat on the floor pressing my back against the wall. Ever since the hockey game, she'd been trying hard not to impose on my time. It only made me feel like a jerk. "You're not a burden, Mom. I love you. I've just been—" My voice caught. I paused, swallowing the lump in my throat. "I've been a little confused."

"Oh, Maddie. Just a second." Something rustled on the speaker. "Okay, I'm sitting down."

I opened the floodgates. I told her my feelings about Chase, the hurt that followed his leaving, my work with the Outlaws and my proposal for the league, then finished with the application sitting on my desk. When I finished, she was quiet a moment.

"I'm a little concerned . . ." she started, and I jumped in.

"About the scholarship? Chase?"

Mom laughed. "The combination of the two. I'd be lying if I said I haven't been thinking about those high school years wondering if I did everything wrong. If I shouldn't have let Chase and his dad move in—"

"Mom, the last thing you need to worry about is me. You went through so much."

"I know, but I never thought—"

"Nothing happened. I just . . . was a little obsessed with him." I winced at the admission.

Mom sighed. "I guess I understand that. He's always been so charming." That was one way to say it. "But now I think I'm more concerned that you're making this choice on the hopes that something will happen with him."

I nodded. "I thought of that too. But I don't think that's it." I'd run the thought experiments, and if Chase didn't ever come back to Calgary, I still wasn't feeling the same excitement about the Rhodes.

"Sometimes dreams are hard work. I don't want you to give up too soon," she mused.

"I know." Again. Same thoughts.

"But . . . " She drew a breath. "I trust you, Maddie. You've always made good decisions for yourself. Sometimes to the point that I wondered if you were human like the rest of us."

I laughed, wiping my eyes.

"It wouldn't be the worst thing to make some mistakes, you know."

A knock sounded at my door, and I jumped. "I make plenty

of mistakes, I promise." I pushed up from the floor. "Mom, Crystal just got here."

"Oh, sure."

"Thank you so much for talking."

"Anytime."

I opened the door and let the phone cord retract. "I love you, Mom." Somehow, while we hadn't come to any conclusions, I felt lighter.

"Love you, too."

I hung up and rushed back to grab my sweatshirt. I would've loved to wear Chase's, but half the guys would recognize it. Plus, I didn't want it to get smoky.

"Ready?" Crystal stood grinning on my step as I swung open the door. "Because she's ready." Crystal held her hands out like Vanna White, and I squealed.

"You didn't tell me it was red!" I grabbed my purse from the side table and ran out to inspect her new car. After a full walk about with appropriate "oohing" and "aahing," I settled into the passenger seat.

Shania Twain thudded through the speakers of Crystal's cherry red 1991 Pontiac Sunbird as we pulled away from the curb. The inside smelled faintly of vanilla air freshener. It had only two working windows and a radio with the tuning knob missing, but Crystal had installed a flower-patterned steering wheel cover and seat beads that clicked when she moved.

"It's amazing!" I called out over the chorus.

She grinned back at me, her hair blowing in the breeze from her cracked window.

It was dusk when we arrived at Nick's family ranch. Our headlights bounced as the sunbird crunched over gravel, spitting up dust. We were fifteen minutes past the last strip of Calgary development, and now it was all wide fields and barbed wire fences.

When we pulled up next to the barn, the yard was already full.

Trucks lined the dirt drive, their tailgates down and stereos low. The smell of grilled burgers mingled with smoke from the bonfire roaring in a pit out back. Strings of mismatched lights were draped between fence posts. Someone had even hauled out a couch.

This was one of many events someone on the team would be hosting over the summer. A night like this is what pulled me into the Outlaws circle in the first place. Shar dragged me to play shinny on Nick's frozen pond during the winter of 1993, and I was hooked.

I walked with Crystal toward the fire where Rob and Shar were tucked into a pair of lawn chairs, her feet on his lap.

As soon as Shar saw us, she swung her legs down and hopped up to greet us both with hugs.

"Your boobs are bigger." I laughed, pulling back to inspect her.

"They totally are," she whisper-laughed. "I told Rob to enjoy it before I have the belly to go with them."

Crystal scoffed. "Whatever, he's going to love that even more."

I glanced over to see Rob watching Shar. He was smitten. Completely and totally wrapped around her finger.

The rest of the night buzzed with games and laughter. The guys got into a heated competition playing tailgate flip cup using a broken hockey stick as a baton. Someone dared Axel to race Bear down the gravel drive on foot, which resulted in a spectacular wipeout and Bear carrying him back fireman-style while everyone howled. Crystal and I dominated at horseshoes, which was really the only important thing to remember.

It was past midnight when the chatter quieted and the group began to thin. Shar stood talking with a friend of Bear's, and Crystal was curled up in the bed of someone's truck with what looked like three other people watching the stars.

Rob and I jumped in to help Nick gather empties and fold up chairs. The fire had dwindled to embers. Bugs whispered in the grass, and the air had that soft chill that meant dew was settling in.

Rob tossed a crumpled paper plate into a garbage bag and nudged a bottle cap with his foot. "You've been busy."

I picked up a folded paper plate. "I know, sorry I haven't been by to help with the nursery set up."

Rob waved me off. "Almost done. You just need to come over and see it."

"No way! I bet Shar's thrilled."

"That she is." He held out the trash bag for me to drop in an empty pack of gum. "What did you end up deciding?"

I blinked, not understanding the question at first. When it clicked, my eyes widened. "Oh, did Shar not tell you? I decided to submit."

His eyebrows shot sky high. "She didn't. When do you find out?"

I grinned. "Found out today. It's approved. I haven't even had a chance to tell Shar yet."

Rob smirked. "Finally. I get an update before she does. When do you start?"

I laughed and picked up a crushed can of Dr. Pepper from under the picnic table. The approval was real. The project was real. The excitement was real too, but underneath it all, a familiar pressure had settled at the base of my chest.

What if no one signed up? Or worse, what if so many people did, we couldn't accommodate them? What if I poured everything into it and then had to walk away in November?

Oxford had always been the dream. The big golden ticket. I'd been shaping my life around it for years. But the idea of leaving, especially now that I had the green light on this project, made my stomach twist. Would I have to drop this and never know if it could have worked?

I shoved the can into the bag and cleared my throat. "Can I ask you something?"

Rob looked over, curious. "Sure."

"How did you do it?" I kept my voice light, but the question felt anything but. "How did you change direction? You worked so hard for that spot on the travel team then gave it up in a second."

He didn't answer right away, just tied off the trash bag. "It took more than a second to make that decision." He walked over and set the bag next to the back corner of the barn. "It felt like a hard decision to make when I took everyone else's ideas into account."

"What do you mean?"

He wiped his hands on his jeans. "Everyone else thought this was the best thing for me. Everyone else had heard me talk about this scouting opportunity, about my dream to push to pro." He exhaled, running a hand through his hair. "Everyone knew Logan had just made it and I hadn't."

I slipped my hands into my back pockets. That sounded familiar.

"But if I let go of that and looked at my own thoughts, it was simple." He shrugged. "The second I saw that pregnancy test, hockey wasn't my dream anymore. So I didn't have to give it up. Just got to start chasing something new."

———

I thanked Crystal for the ride—it felt so weird that she was driving me now—and hurried inside my apartment. The lights were off, so I slipped off my shoes and crept down the hall, not wanting to wake anyone.

In my room, the glow from the streetlight edged past the curtains and painted a bright line across my desk. And there they were. Exactly where I'd left them: the Rhodes application on one side, the proposal from Lamont on the other.

Dropping my purse next to the chair, I sat on the edge of the bed and closed my eyes. What I would've given to have Chase there running a hand up my arm, telling my mind to be still. I did the best I could in his absence, forcing myself to notice the quilt beneath my palms, the carpet under my feet.

"No, thank you," I whispered to the hundreds of thoughts still clamouring for attention, raising a din over the past two weeks. Being with Chase didn't solve my overthinking completely, but simply knowing there was another option was enough to make me stronger.

I could do this, at least in part. As my mind settled, I listened to Rob's advice. *What did I think?*

I'm not sure how long I sat there, but once the clouds began to part, it was exactly as Rob described.

Easy.

I turned on the desk lamp and sat down, pulling out a fresh sheet of paper. I started with Chase's name, then let everything pour out of me.

When I finished, I set the pen down and picked up my application, sealed in its envelope. Then, I dropped it into the trash.

Thirty

AT THE END OF JULY, I stood at the edge of the ice under the Dome with a clipboard in my hand and only a small pit in my stomach. The lights buzzed overhead. I'd never seen the ice from this angle behind the bench.

The bleachers were mostly empty—just a handful of friends and volunteers—but the players were already trickling in, sticks in their hands, duffels, skates, and helmets slung over their shoulders.

I'd started with Douglas alumni, working from a list of emails and phone numbers Lamont provided. We had enough for two full rosters, and this was our first official scrimmage.

Crystal handed out name tags Sharpied onto pieces of masking tape. I was positive she'd offered to take this job specifically so she could check out all the players. It was a baller move.

Sharla and Rob couldn't be there, but they'd contacted over a third of my initial list. To my surprise, Blakely and Kaplan both showed up tonight. I'd made it clear I didn't expect them to coach, but having them here allowed me to stop wearing my shoulders as earrings.

At seven o'clock, I cleared my throat and stepped into the group of players near the benches. "Alright, everyone, thanks for coming. You're here because you love the game and don't want it to end just because school or life or careers got in the way. As I mentioned on the phone and over email, this league isn't built yet. Today's a scrimmage, but my goal is to make this high level and competitive. That said, we're going to build it together, so whatever it becomes, it'll reflect you. Your needs, your voices, your goals. I have some basic logistics here—game dates, draft ideas, tiers depending on skill level. But nothing is set in stone. If this works, it's because *we* make it work."

A few heads nodded. One guy with long curls raised a hand. "Does the league have a name?"

I hesitated, glancing at Crystal. I hadn't said these particular words out loud to anyone, not wanting to jinx it. "I was thinking the Elite League."

The guys nodded, tapping their sticks on the concrete. The energy shifted. Excitement buzzed like static electricity. Guys slapping each other on the back, tapping sticks, pointing out old teammates across the room.

"Alright. Get changed. Let's get on the ice."

As the guys hustled to the locker rooms, I turned to Kaplan. I'd guzzled my entire bottle of water and hadn't taken a second to use the washroom. "Scrimmage teams are posted by the east door. First face-off is in thirty. Can you get them warming up?."

He nodded, and I jogged down the corridor toward the back hallway. I turned the corner and ran into something solid.

I gasped, stumbling back, but strong hands caught my elbows. "I'm so—" Every cell in my body stood on its head.

Chase.

His hair was longer than the last time I'd seen him, brushing the tops of his ears. His grey tee hugged his chest and shoulders. His eyes were warm, a little tired, but soft in a way that made me think of Clearwater.

My breath slipped. "You got my letter."

Chase's brows drew together. "I haven't gotten a letter in a couple of weeks."

I opened my mouth, then closed it. How long ago had I sent it? Definitely not weeks ago. But if he hadn't gotten it . . . "But you're here."

He nodded, looping his thumbs in the belt loops of his jeans, then thinking better of it and crossing his arms. "I caught your speech."

My eyes widened. "You were here?"

He nodded. "In the stands."

My cheeks flushed. "It wasn't really a speech. Just logistics."

There was the exhale followed by the eye drop. My heart fluttered, waiting for the smile that came next.

"This is amazing, Maddie. I'm so proud of you." He glanced up, peering at me through his dark lashes.

"Is that why you came back? To tell me that?" My hands tingled. I didn't want to seem impatient, but not knowing why Chase was standing in front of me gave me heart palpitations. He hadn't gotten my letter, which meant he didn't know how I felt. Writing it was one thing, but I didn't think I had the courage to say it to his face. Especially when I didn't know if—

"I moved back," Chase said in a rush.

The words sank into me in layers. "You—what?"

Chase smiled, a little crooked, a little unsure. "I'm back in Calgary. I'm coming back to coach."

My eyes flooded without warning. I blinked to clear them, then pressed my lips together. He was coming back? Relief and hesitation rushed through me in equal measures. All I'd thought of was Chase coming back, but in every scenario I envisioned—I was becoming a master at fantasies—he and I were together. But if he was coming back to coach . . .

We'd have to keep things professional, keep our distance. The thought of that made my chest feel like it was caving in on itself. And he didn't know I'd decided against the Rhodes, so maybe him coming back had nothing to do with me in the first place. Maybe he was here because of Blakely and Kaplan.

Chase's smile faltered. "Maddie, I thought you'd be happy. I hoped—" He took a step closer and pulled me to him. "What the hell was in that letter?"

I shook my head, lifting a hand to his chest. "I don't think I can do that again. I'm so glad you're back, but if you're going to be working here—I have one year left—"

"One year? I thought you only had six months."

The tears came faster. He wasn't here because of me. My heart split at the seams, and I couldn't stop my shoulders from shaking.

"Hey. I'm not coming back to Douglas. Is that what you're upset about?" He pulled back and lifted his hand to my face. His thumb brushed the tear that slipped past my cheekbone.

"What?"

"I'm not coaching here."

"But you just said—"

"I said I was coming back to coach. I didn't say *where*." He reached into his back pocket, pulled out an envelope, and handed it to me.

I took it with shaking fingers and opened the flap. A single-page letter, printed on official letterhead.

Calgary Hitmen Hockey Club

Dear Coach Wilson,

We are pleased to formally offer you a position as an assistant coach with the Calgary Hitmen organization. Your experience as a player, your track record mentoring young athletes, and your recent work with the Douglas University Outlaws make you an exceptional candidate . .

.

I stared at the letter, then at him.

He cleared his throat. "You once asked me what I wanted."

I stood, stunned, waiting for him to continue.

It took him a moment to gather his thoughts. "I thought I wanted to never hurt again. To never put my eggs in any basket so I couldn't be disappointed. What I didn't realize was that holding my eggs didn't save me from pain or disappointment." He winced. "That metaphor didn't sound as good out loud as it did inside my head."

I laughed, swiping another tear from my cheek, making sure it didn't land on the letter.

"Trying to accept my life without you in it or sitting back and waiting to see if it works out is making me miserable. So maybe you'll tell me you don't want this thing between us, or maybe you'll go off to England and find someone or something better, but—"

"I'm not going to England."

Chase frowned. "You've already heard back? I thought applications just opened."

I folded the letter and handed it back to him. "I'm not going because I'm not submitting my application."

Chase's frown deepened. "Maddie, I didn't come here to convince you—"

"If you would've read my damn letter you'd know that I let go of that dream before you ever showed up."

Chase returned the letter to his back pocket. "Okay."

"I was able to get this project approved through Lamont. It's for credit, and I want to see it through. But this is all beside the point because you're here and you're not a faculty member anymore, and I think what you're saying is that you came back because of me, which I'm really hoping is true because the other bit of info I gave in that letter is that I love you." I sucked in a breath, my head spinning. I couldn't believe I just said it.

A muscle in Chase's jaw jumped. His breathing quickened as he looked over my shoulder, then reached out and grabbed my wrist as he walked, pulling me with him. He pushed through the visiting team's locker room door, and the second it clicked shut behind us, Chase spun and kissed me.

I melted into him like ice cream on a hot day as he eased me back against the first bank of lockers, one hand around my waist, the other bracing himself against the metal.

"What about Vancouver?" I breathed against his mouth.

"I never officially accepted. Went out for a tour and declined," he rasped, already hunting for my jaw, my neck. "I never let go of my lease here. Couldn't bring myself to do it."

Warmth bubbled through me. "You wanted to stay."

He smiled, his teeth brushing my collarbone. "I was in denial."

I thought about the weeks that my Rhodes application had sat on my nightstand. I knew a thing or two about that.

His mouth found mine again, his fingers tangling in my hair. I tugged him closer by the front of his shirt. "While I would love to stay here all night, I *do* have to get back to the league at some point."

He sighed, his lips slowing. "How late will it go?"

"Two hours max."

Chase lifted his arm and checked his watch. "We're already twenty-five minutes in." He breathed heavily, still clutching me against him. "Meet me in the lobby after?"

My heart skipped a beat. "Sure."

His nostrils flared. "Yes, please."

CHAPTER
Thirty~One

I'D BEEN MOTIVATED to end the game on time. After talking with the guys and gratefully accepting Coach Blakely's offer to wait around until the players left the building, I bolted up the stairs to the main floor of the Dome. Chase was leaning against the wall, waiting.

"Does Blakely know you're here?" I asked.

His mouth curled. "Possibly."

That explained Coach's eagerness to send me off. For a second, I was embarrassed about what he might assume we were doing together, but I pushed the thoughts away. I was getting good at that.

Without another word, Chase straightened and strode toward me, scooping my hand into his. We walked to the parking lot, then split into our vehicles. Instead of searching for his address again, I opted to follow.

I only got stopped at one red light on the way, and he graciously waited for me, only pissing off a few drivers in the process.

We pulled up to the curb. I parked, then met him in front of the walkway to his home. Chase threw an arm over my shoulders and we strode together to the door.

"You smell good," I murmured.

Chase chuckled. He unlocked the door, nudged it open, then pulled me toward the stairs. After a brief pause to lock the deadbolt and flick on a light, we ascended.

The floorboards creaked under our feet, and when we reached the landing, he directed me right, toward the door at the end of the hall.

"Do you have anything in the morning?" Chase asked.

My stomach, which was already doing somersaults, took another flip for good measure. "No. I don't work until one. You?" My whole body shivered.

Chase clicked on a lamp, and I scanned his room. It felt like I was discovering more pieces of him as I took in the clean lines and uncluttered space. There was a dresser and a chair in the corner, and a queen bed with crisp, white linens. The navy comforter sat slightly rumpled, like he'd sat there on the bed at some point that day.

"I'm free. You okay?" he asked, his voice low.

I nodded. I didn't trust myself to speak. My pulse was already thudding like a bass drum. He stepped closer, one hand brushing my arm, trailing down until our fingers met again.

"I keep thinking I'm going to wake up," I whispered.

Chase's lips lifted at one corner. "You're not dreaming."

But I was. I had to be. This version of him—barefoot, tousled —he didn't exist in real life. Not this gentle. Not this undone. He looked like a wish I hadn't dared to make.

This time, I was positive Chase moved first. I rose on my tiptoes as he pressed a light kiss to my mouth. He cupped my waist and pulled me toward the bed. "Lie down."

I nodded again, but before I could crawl on top of his mattress, he tugged at my shirt. At my pants.

"Oh, did you want these off?" I teased.

His eyes glazed. "Yes, please."

I moved slowly, enjoying the widening of his pupils as I removed my shirt and pants, then sat on the bed. I pulled myself to the middle and lay back on his pillows. Chase stood there, watching.

After a moment, he stripped off his shirt and dropped his jeans to the floor, kicking both articles of clothing out of the way, then climbed up onto the bed with me. He settled above me, and his mouth started on my stomach, right beneath my ribs.

I sucked in a breath.

"Do you like this?" His voice was low, his breath warming my skin.

"Yes."

He flicked his tongue over my lowest rib, then kissed his way to the underwire of my bra. "Where else do you want me to touch?"

It was only the second time he'd asked that, and I was already in love with the question. It made me feel like he trusted me. Like he expected me to know the answer.

I threaded my fingers in his hair, and when he looked up, my cheeks heated at the devilish grin on his face. "Surprise me," I murmured.

If tonight was any indication, Chase was good at surprises.

I tilted my head back, eyes fluttering shut. Every brush of his lips sent sparks chasing down my spine. I let my hands roam over his warm skin, reacquainting myself with my favourite parts of him.

"I'm so glad you're staying." Chase made his way back to my mouth. He lowered himself against me, dipping his leg between mine. I traced my hand over his cheekbone, his jaw. "I love you, Maddie girl."

I grinned. "I doubt Axel is going to let you coin that."

His eyes darkened as he smoothed my hair over his pillow. "I think you'll hear it a little differently out of my mouth."

Heat flashed across my thighs. "I'll need a sample to compare."

Chase kissed my forehead, my temple, my nose. "Did you bring a notebook?"

I laughed, wrapping my arms around his neck. No more watching on the deck. Tonight we were diving into the deep end. "I always bring a notebook."

"Good. Because you're going to want to write this down." Chase slipped the strap of my bra off my shoulder, and my breath shook as I closed my eyes and *felt*.

Somehow, after months of dedicated research, all the puzzle pieces fell into place. I knew this man, and more importantly, I knew who I was with him.

Maybe love didn't follow a proof. Maybe this particular equation didn't balance until we both stopped trying to solve it.

Chase murmured, "Perfect symmetry," against my skin, followed by, "Absolute maximum curvature." I breathed a laugh, but he didn't let me respond. He brushed a hand over my thigh. "And your legs? Optimal slope."

I sighed, grasping his shoulders. "I'll never be glad this is over." I murmured, sucking his earlobe into my mouth.

"What?" he asked on a laugh.

"Nothing." I grinned, breathing him in. From the moment I'd stepped into Room 413, I knew I'd never be the woman in that poem with Chase.

"I love you," I whispered into his neck. "We're so good at this already."

Epilogue

Crystal

STREAMERS IN PINK and blue twisted between the old wooden beams of Ranchman's. Sharla was perched on a stool opening presents. She looked beautiful—round-bellied and flushed. Rob stood behind her like he was her personal guard dog, grinning each time she turned to put a baby item on display.

There was food, laughter, and a game of pin the cord on the belly button. Axel made the point that the goal was to remove the cord after birth, but Rob told him the goal was steadiness of hand, then proceeded to spin him ten times before letting him loose.

It was perfect. Which was why, after taking a small piece of cake, I was ready to head home.

I made the rounds, embracing my friends. I spent a little time chatting with Maddie and Chase, who had decided that after so much time apart, they no longer wished to stop touching each other, then made my way to the street.

My car was parked a half a block down. I held my purse tight and started toward the crosswalk, but didn't make it.

The truck in front of me was familiar. I paused, staring at it, then jumped when the driver's side door opened.

Holy shit.

"Hey, Logan." I crossed my arms, trying not to show my shock. What was he doing here? Why was he sitting out here in front of Ranchman's in the dark?

"Hey." He ran a hand over the back of his neck.

My shoulders dropped a centimetre. "She would've wanted you to come in."

He shrugged. "Felt weird. I'm happy for her and Rob, don't get me wrong—"

"No, I get it." I put myself in his shoes. He'd only been gone six months and his ex was engaged and pregnant. Ouch.

Logan glanced at the Ranchman's sign. "Why are you leaving so early?"

I scoffed. "Baby showers aren't exactly ragers."

His mouth curved at the edges, and I was glad for the moment of normalcy between us. I hadn't ever hated Logan, but I didn't like who Shar was when she was with him.

"Maddie has a boyfriend?" Logan asked.

I exhaled. Well. He cut right to the quick. While I'd loved being with my friends, in the last week, I'd become their fifth wheel. It was better to take off before it was so obvious it became embarrassing.

"How long are you in town for?" I asked, ignoring his question. If he wanted more details, he'd have to walk through that door.

"Uh . . ." He gave a nervous smile. "Indefinitely. I'm playing with the Blizzard."

My jaw dropped. "You . . . what?"

He smiled, and a little of the old Logan sprang to life. "Yep, kind of exciting. I wanted to tell the guys, but it seems like they're more of a package deal now."

Logan took a step back toward his truck. "Will you let me know when the baby comes? I feel weird asking Rob, but I wanted to get them something. "

Something in my chest tugged. "Mmhmm. Sure." I pulled out a pen from my purse. "What's your number?" Logan rattled off the digits, and I wrote them on my palm.

He thanked me, then gave a little wave and got in the truck. His taillights blinked red, and just as he pulled away from the curb, the door opened to Ranchman's.

"What are you doing?" Maddie yelled. "She's about to open your gift!"

I groaned internally. What was I supposed to tell her? That I'd left and decided to walk so slowly to my car, I was still directly across the street? "Just getting some air."

Maddie pushed the door further, waving for me to come back in.

I glanced up the street, but Logan's truck was long gone. I started back toward the door, taking one last look at the numbers on my skin and slipping the pen back into my purse.

I wasn't going to tell Maddie or Shar about seeing Logan, not tonight. It could wait for the next girl's night.

"I think you're too independent with your own car," Maddie teased. "How are we supposed to force you to stay longer than you want?"

I laughed. "Looks like you've still got it figured out."

Maddie threw her arm around me and pulled me back into the pub.

$$Epilogue\ 2$$

Maddie's letter, postmarked July 28th, 1995. Arrived return to sender September 16, 1995 and immediately read by Chase Wilson.

Chase,

I'm sorry it took me so long to write. I've been doing a lot of thinking, too. When we met, I was dead-set on applying for the Rhodes, and I know right now you're yelling at this paper saying "You're still going to apply for that damn scholarship" so don't hate me for what I'm about to say next.

I'm not going to submit. Not because of you, so you can breathe easy. I realize that you've committed to your job in Vancouver and it's probably unlikely that the two of us will cross paths in any long-term way anytime soon. That breaks my heart a little. I didn't say anything when you left, not because I didn't want to, but because you'd made it clear that you didn't want to try.

So here goes. This is my best attempt at explaining the thousand things running through my head in some sort of conglomeration that makes sense.

I think I love you. There. Got that out of the way. You told me once that wanting doesn't make a difference. That it either is or it isn't. To that I say (as you taught me), "No thank you." Wanting makes all the difference, and here's my proof:

Before we met (again) I wanted the Rhodes. It pushed me to work my hardest academically, but also to search for some way I could serve and make a difference. If I hadn't wanted that, I never would've walked into your office. I never would've said yes to serve on the committee, and I never would've discovered new pieces of myself in the study room while trying to explain differential equations, or in that hotel room in Clearwater.

And not wanting makes all the difference, too. Did you know I've heard from three other guys on the Outlaws that you helped them with something? Nick's car, Tim's textbook fees, and a donation to Rob when he bought that ring for Sharla. You didn't want your guys to suffer, so you helped them in ways you absolutely didn't need to. I hope you know they love you for it. Axel mopes around like a wounded puppy talking about how much it sucks you won't be back for Kaplan in the fall.

I'm better because I wanted. Which leads me to my final point.

The whole reason I wanted the Rhodes? I've been staring down graduation with no idea what I was going to do with a math degree. You and I aren't so different. We both worked our hardest to follow the "one" path we were supposed to. Yours ended a bit earlier, but I would've been sitting there with you in another year.

Maybe I would've found direction going to Oxford, but because I wanted—and because you wanted to be a good coach (and possibly to spend time with me . . . I'd be lying if I didn't hope that was part of your motivation), I found direction here.

I've already met with Kowalski and Lamont, and I've been approved to start a project I'm calling the Elite League Initiative. (If you hate it, tell me. Not sure it'll stick.) It's a partnership between the math department and athletics, and it's going to serve as my independent research project for senior credit.

The idea is to create a sustainable post-collegiate hockey league for players who age out of Juniors or university play but don't move on to the minors or NHL. I'm using practical mathematical analysis and predictive modeling to study player longevity, cost-efficiency, and long-term participation metrics.

It's small right now. Just a few scrimmages. I'm hoping I'll get enough guys to show up. But it's already changing how I see things. I used to think math was only about answers. Equations. Certainty. But the truth is, I love the messy parts. The unpredictable human variables. That's what makes the numbers matter.

And Chase, you were the variable I didn't see coming.

You nudged me outside of my comfort zone. Made me ask different questions. Ones I didn't know how to solve.

Thank you for being unpredictable. For not making sense. Maybe not a typical compliment, but I hope you'll take it as such.

So, dear sir, I call bullshit on your thesis. The numbers don't add up. While it's scary as hell to admit all of this, I don't want to stop wanting.

Love Maddie

P.S. I'll open the door in underwear and a T-shirt for you anytime, and at some point, I'd love to see them in a pile on your floor.

NEXT IN THE SERIES: THE COMEBACK

Crystal knows getting tangled up with Logan is a terrible idea. He broke her best friend's heart, and she swore she'd never be the girl who forgave him.

But when Logan's connection lands her an interview with a major Calgary art icon, pretending to be his girlfriend suddenly feels like a small price to pay for her dream job.

What starts as a fake-dating favor quickly spirals into something very real—especially when a PR weekend in Banff blurs every line they promised not to cross.

Tropes:
- Fake Dating
- Secret Romance
- Slow Burn
- Tight-Knit Friend Group
- Found Family
- Snarky Banter

Click here to buy Book #3 in the Canadian Played series!

Douglas University
Campus Directory

Spring 1995 Edition

GRB Science Complex

Named for Dr. Gwendolyn Rae Bell, one of Alberta's first female chemists and a fierce advocate for women in science.

Home to the university's science, engineering, and medical studies, the GRB includes:

- **Abbott Hall** – *Named for Dr. Maude Abbott,* a pioneering cardiologist and medical researcher. Houses Biology, Pre-Med, and Health Sciences.
- **Elijah McCoy Wing** – *Named for inventor Elijah McCoy,* who revolutionized steam engine lubrication. This wing houses Engineering and Innovation.
- **Carrie Derick Pavilion** – *Named for botanist and early geneticist Carrie Derick,* Canada's first female university professor. Home to Psychology and Gender Studies.

- **Sandford Fleming Basement Labs** – *Named for engineer Sandford Fleming*, who invented standard time zones. Physics, Applied Math, and advanced computation are tucked down here.

Coxeter Building

Named for Donald Coxeter, world-renowned Canadian mathematician celebrated for his work on geometry, symmetry, and polytopes.

This building houses pure and applied mathematics, with upper-level lecture halls and quiet problem-solving lounges tucked under high arched windows.

McCoy Centre for Innovation and Engineering

Named for Elijah McCoy, Black Canadian-American inventor with over 50 patents.

A standalone modern building for engineering, applied technology, and interdisciplinary research, formerly part of the GRB Complex.

Rozsa Arts Centre & Concert Hall

Named for Helen Rozsa, philanthropist and advocate for the arts in Western Canada.

A creative hub for music, visual arts, and theatre. Connected to the GRB via an underground tunnel.

- **Pauline Johnson Hall** – *Named for Mohawk-English poet E. Pauline Johnson*, who fused Indigenous storytelling with Victorian verse. A 600-seat venue for concerts and productions.
- Also includes gallery space, music rehearsal halls, and studio classrooms.

Main Quad & Academic Halls

- **Peter Lougheed Centre** – *Named for Alberta Premier Peter Lougheed*, who reshaped provincial rights and oil policy. Faculty of Law, Policy, and Resource Management.
- **Irene Parlby Hall** – *Named for suffragist and politician Irene Parlby*, one of the Famous Five. Houses Political Science and Public Health.
- **Emily Stowe Building** – *Named for Dr. Emily Stowe*, Canada's first woman doctor and a women's rights advocate. Liberal Arts and the Student Wellness Office.
- **Agnes Macphail Commons** – *Named for MP Agnes Macphail*, the first woman in Parliament. Student government offices, club rooms, and media centre.
- **James Gladstone Centre** – *Named for Canada's first Indigenous senator, James Gladstone (Blood/Kainai)*. Indigenous Policy and Environmental Sustainability.

Student Residences & Community Spaces

- **Agnes Macphail Commons** – *Named for Agnes Macphail*, first woman elected to Canada's House of

Commons. The university's oldest residence hall. Now houses dormitories, student government offices, campus media rooms, and social lounges.

- **Partridge House** – *Named for Margaret Partridge*, a pioneering female electrical engineer who advocated for women in trades and science. A co-ed upper-year dorm known for its independent vibe, quiet study zones, and legendary third-floor potlucks.

Athletics & Student Life

- **Douglas Dome** – Modern ice arena and home of the *Douglas Outlaws*. Hosts varsity hockey and regional tournaments.
- **The North Centre** – Includes fitness facilities, a pool, and climbing wall for student use.

About the Author

Cindy Gunderson is a voice actress and award-winning author. Since she has commitment issues, she writes both sci-fi and fantasy, as well as contemporary romance and women's fiction under the pen name, Cynthia Gunderson.

When she is not typing away in a quiet corner of her local library, you can find her traveling with her family, narrating audiobooks, or happily digging in her garden. She loves acting and performing, beating her kids in card games, and playing ultimate frisbee with her handsome husband, Scott.

Cindy grew up in Alberta, Canada, but has lived most of her adult life between California and Colorado. She currently resides in the Denver metro area. Cindy holds a B.S. in Psychology from Brigham Young University.

Cindy's first novel Tier 1 was awarded First Place in Science Fiction at the 2021 CIPPA EVVY Awards and her women's fiction novel Yes, And was honored with the Indie Author Award's first place prize for the state of Colorado, 2023.